Romance of the SNOB SQUAD

JULIE ANNE PETERS

LITTLE, BROWN AND COMPANY
New York | Boston

Little, Brown and Company

Hachette Book Group
237 Park Avenue, New York, NY 10017
Visit our website at www.lb-kids.com

Little, Brown and Company is a division of Hachette Book Group, Inc.
The Little, Brown name and logo are trademarks of Hachette Book Group, Inc.

First Revised Paperback Edition: January 2010
First published in hardcover in 1999 by Little, Brown and Company

The characters and events portrayed in this book are fictitious. Any similarity
to real persons, living or dead, is coincidental and not intended by the author.

Library of Congress Cataloging-in-Publication Data

Peters, Julie Anne
    Romance of the Snob Squad / by Julie Anne Peters. — 1st ed.
    p.   cm.
    Sequel to: Revenge of the Snob Squad
    Summary: Sixth-grade misfits Jenny, Max, Prairie, and Lydia plot
    to ignite a romance between Prairie and the object of her affection,
    Hugh Torkerson, otherwise known as Tork the Dork.
      ISBN 978-0-316-70627-8 (HC) / ISBN 978-0-316-00813-6 (PB)
      [1. Schools — Fiction.] I. Title.
PZ7.P44158Ro   1999
[Fic] — dc21   97-40787

10 9 8 7 6 5 4 3 2 1

RRD-C

Printed in the United States of America

To love,
a many-splendored thing

Chapter 1

"Truth or dare." My index finger circled the group and stopped on . . . "Prairie." She flinched. The four of us, the Snob Squad, were hanging out after school, doing what we usually did. Avoiding homework.

"T-truth," Prairie said.

I popped a sunflower seed into my mouth and sucked off the salt, thinking up a question. "Okay, try this. Who are you in love with?"

"Ooh." Lydia scootched around to face Prairie. "Good one, Jenny."

Max said, "Anyone got a Coke? I'm dying of thirst here."

"I have a can of Slim Fast," I told her.

Max looked mortified. Then, clucking in resignation, she held out her hand. I dug in my backpack to find it.

"Come on, Prairie," Lydia said. "Tell us who you love."

Prairie's face turned pink. In a tiny voice she said, "Hugh T-Torkerson."

"Hugh Torkerson!" Lydia scootched back fast. "That nerd? You're in love with Hugh Torkerson?"

"Hey." Max shot Lydia full of eye bullets. "It's her love, not yours."

"Thank gawd." Lydia stuck out her tongue.

Max sneered at Lydia, then slugged down my whole can of Slim Fast. Rats. I was saving that for dessert. "Hugh's not so bad," I lied.

Hugh was the nerdiest guy in the whole sixth grade. His nickname was Tork the Dork. He mumbled to himself. He scratched his pits. And he had a laugh like Lydia's, loud and obnoxious. The hyena howl, I called it. Hugh resembled Max, sort of. A big bruiser, except whereas Max was muscular and athletic, Hugh was just huge. Even though he was a computer nerd, I always thought Hugh Torkerson was mentally challenged.

Maybe that was Prairie's attraction. Not that she

lacked brainpower. No way. Prairie had other disabil-
ities. Her stuttering for one thing. And the deformed
leg she was born with.

"Hugh Torkerson," Lydia repeated, shaking her
head. "Heaven help us." She prayed to the rusty
ceiling.

"Truth," Max said to Lydia. "You love Nick
Claussen." To the rest of us, she added, "He's this
flunky fourth grader who lives down the street."

"I do not!" Lydia cried. "Anyway"—she blushed
bright as cherry Jell-O—"Nick Claussen is very
mature for his age."

"Oh, yeah." Max spat a sunflower shell out the
cracked window. "He's mature all right. I saw him
picking his nose at a soccer game last week. Guess he
got bored being goalie."

"Or hungry," I said.

"You guys." Lydia sneered.

Max, Prairie, and I exchanged smirks. It wasn't our
habit to torment Lydia Beals, but it sure was fun.

Lydia said, "Truth or dare." Her narrowed eyes
shifted from Max to me. "Jenny."

I jumped. Which was more dangerous? Consider-
ing the consequences of either, I said, "Let's do something else."

"Like what?" Lydia said.

"I know." Max crossed one army boot over her knee. "Let's play strip poker."

Lydia's eyes popped out. "You're insane."

I elbowed Lydia. "She's kidding." To Max I said, "You are kidding, aren't you?"

Lounging back in her beanbag chair, Max just grinned.

"Forget it," I said. "I don't want to get arrested." Good thing I was leader of the Snob Squad and not Max. We'd have been holed up in a holding cell downtown instead of hanging out in the Peacemobile.

The Peacemobile is our secret meeting place. It's a rusty old minivan that Max's brother, Scuzz-Gut, permanently parked in his junkyard. Excuuuse me, his used auto parts establishment. The van's called the Peacemobile because someone, a former flower child from the love generation, pasted peace signs all over it.

"What else you got to eat, Solano?" Max said.

At the bottom of my backpack was a crushed box. I yanked it out. "This is it, folks. Low-fat granola bars."

Max snatched the green box, ripped it open at the wrong end, and helped herself. Then she passed around the mutilated box.

"How's your diet coming?" Lydia asked, dropping granola bars all over the floor. Lydia's a total klutz.

"It's not a diet," I reminded her. "It's a nutrition plan. And you had to ask, didn't you?" I took one bite of granola bar and gagged. "I'd give my left leg for a Little Debbie."

"Don't say that!" Lydia gasped. She motioned with her chin to Prairie's foot.

"Sorry." My face seared. "Make that Ashley Krupps's left leg."

"Jenny." Prairie kicked me with her prosthesis.

We all sniggered. Ashley Krupps was our arch-enemy. Over the years she'd hounded and humiliated each of us, which had forged a common bond among us. That's how we became the Snob Squad. As a team, we vowed to take revenge on Ashley Krupps. But that was last month. That was history. You know what they say, though. History tends to repeat itself.

After the granola bars got around, Lydia said, "What is your nutrition plan, Jenny?"

"Basically I have to keep this food diary," I explained. "I have to write down everything that passes through my lips."

"Including air?" Max smirked.

What a wit. "Yeah, if I suck in one calorie, it goes in the book."

Max crunched her granola bar. "Major drag."

"Tell me about it."

"You l-look thinner alr-ready," Prairie said.

That's what I liked about Prairie. Even when she lied, it was heartfelt.

Max finished her granola bar in one gulp and fisted the wrapper. In a garble she added, "You were never fat, if you ask me."

And that's what I liked about Max. She lied like a pro. I turned to Lydia. She gave me a sick smile and shrugged. Oh, well. Two out of three. Lydia scootched around to sit facing me, Indian style. "So, who do *you* love, Jenny?" she said in a singsong. "As if we didn't know."

I choked on my granola bar, and not because it had the texture of gravel. They couldn't know. Nobody knew. "Uh, who do you think?" I swallowed hard.

Lydia grinned. "It's obvious. Isn't it, guys?"

They looked blank to me.

Lydia clucked. "Mr. Vance, of course."

Mr. Vance was the new music teacher. Very young. Very sexy, if you like tall, dark, and hairy as an ape. Personally, I pass. But just about every girl in the sixth grade had a crush on Mr. Vance. I thought he smelled suspiciously of bananas. "Boy, Lyd." I snapped my fingers in front of her face. "Nothin' gets past you."

She beamed.

My true secret love was Kevin Rooney. He was a god. Unfortunately, Melanie Mason worshiped him, too. Which narrowed my chances to less than absolute zero. Given a choice between lardo legs Jenny Solano and supermodel Melanie Mason, even I'd pick her.

Prairie sighed. "I wish Hugh would ask me to the s-sixth-grade s-spring fling."

We all stared at her. The only girls who actually got *asked* to the dance were those in relationships. You know, going together? Couples? Which numbered two this week.

"M-maybe I'll ask him," she said.

We all dropped jaws. The only girls who asked guys were . . . you know.

Lydia blurted, "The only girls who ask guys to the dance are sluts." They don't call Lydia Bealsqueal for nothing. She added, "There's got to be a way to get Hugh to ask you." She looked at me. "Doesn't there?"

"Don't look at me," I said. "Has he ever talked to you, Prairie? Have you talked to him?" I shuddered at the thought.

"N-no," she said.

"Thank gawd for that," Lydia muttered.

"Who could get a word in edgewise anyway?" I asked.

They laughed. Apparently they knew Hugh's habits, too. It isn't so weird, talking to yourself. Everyone does it occasionally. Don't they? Except Hugh mumbled out loud at all-school assemblies, in the lunch line, during silent reading. Come on, shut up.

Lydia leaped to her feet. "That's a good idea, Jenny."

"What is?"

"Getting Hugh to ask Prairie to the dance. I bet if we put our heads together, we can come up with a plan. After all"— she smiled —"we are the Snob Squad. All for one and one for all." She proffered the Snob Squad salute. Finger to nose to Ashley.

"You r-really think we c-can?" Prairie's eyes lit up.

"You bet." Lydia rubbed her hands together. "This is so exciting. Okay, Jenny, what's the plan?"

"Plan? I don't have a plan." Truth was I didn't have a clue how to get two people together. If I did, think I'd have been lounging around there with Kevin Rooney on the loose?

A car honked out front. Prairie scrambled to her feet. "That's p-probably my mom. She's picking me up for a doctor's appointment." She headed toward the sliding door. It used to slide. Max helped her heave it open against the rust. Before leaving, Prairie turned and said, "You c-can't tell Hugh how I f-feel.

I'd d-die. And he c-can't know what we're doing, either. It has to be a s-secret plan."

"Right," we agreed. Secret was our middle name.

Prairie clunked down off the Peacemobile. "Ouch," she said under her breath. But we all heard her. Lydia and I rushed to the door.

"You okay?" Max asked.

"F fine."

She said fine, but she hobbled away, like it hurt.

Lydia flopped back down on the flowered sofa, raising decades-old dust mites. "This isn't going to be easy," she said. "And we only have four weeks before the dance." She pushed her glasses up her nose and smiled. "Let's call it Operation Love in the Afternoon."

She'd been watching too many soaps. Max groaned, echoing my sentiments. "How about Rope a Dope," I suggested.

Max snorted.

That encouraged me. "Operation Herd a Nerd?"

"Perfect!" Lydia tapped an index finger against her chin. "And I know just what we need to do first."

Max and I exchanged worried glances. One word crossed my mind: *uh-oh*. Or is that two words?

Chapter 2

Mom was in the kitchen making dinner when I got home. Usually Dad played Mr. Mom and did all the cooking. Except now that I was on a nutrition plan, Mom had taken over dinner duty. I thought Dad's cooking was bad, but Mom's concoctions made his meat loaf taste like gourmet cuisine.

"Hi, Jenny." She smiled at me over the spatula as she flipped a hamburger. Wait. A hamburger isn't supposed to smell like burnt oatmeal. Oh, no. Not veggie burgers again. "How was your club meeting?" Mom asked.

I forced a grim grin. "Swell. We made leather holsters to sell to the gangs at school."

Mom still thought the Snob Squad was a girls'

club, like Scouts or Bluebirds. She had hopes that one day I'd be normal, like my sister, Vanessa. Well, maybe Vanessa isn't the best example.

"Where's Dad?" Under my breath, I added, "Picking up a family bucket at KFC, I hope."

Mom heard me and scowled. "He's downstairs practicing." The sound hit me then, the twang of a banjo, the clomp of boots. Mom and Dad were taking two-stepping lessons. You know, country dancing? It was part of their plan to save their marriage. Unfortunately, it was wrecking their relationship with their children. Speaking of which . . . "Where's psycho sis?" I asked.

"Jenny!" Now a major scowl darkened Mom's face. "Really."

Sufficiently chastised, I popped a pickle into my mouth. "Sorry. Where is the lovely and charming Vanessa? Wait. Don't tell me." Over the screech of a yodel from the basement below, the strains of Mozart wafted down the hall. Or was it Benny Goodman? "She's practicing *again*?"

Mom exhaled a long breath.

"For how long already?"

She glanced up at the kitchen clock. "About forty-five minutes."

"Long enough," I said. "It's time for the support

team to intervene." Bust that stupid clarinet over her sicko head, is what I meant.

My sister and I were both addicts. Vanessa was addicted to the clarinet, among other things. A bejillion other things, not including the one thing I was addicted to. Food. Junk food, to be specific.

I headed for Vanessa's room. Mom called after me, "Your father and I have line dancing lessons tonight, so dinner's in ten minutes. Tell Vanessa. And Jenny, don't forget to write that pickle down in your food diary."

Sure, Mom, I thought. Right above my entry for the Hostess cupcakes I have hidden in my underwear drawer and plan to enjoy as my main course.

I knocked on Vanessa's door. No answer, as usual. Who could hear over Benny Goodman? "Van?" I cracked the door. She sat upright on a cold, steel folding chair, her music stand propped in front of her. Through chipmunk cheeks she blew into her clarinet. Thanks to Vanessa, I'd come to despise the clarinet. All band instruments, actually.

Clapping my hands over my ears, I charged in and ripped the music off her stand. She continued playing for a few seconds until her eyes deglazed. "Hey!"

I pointed to my watch. "Torture time is up."

She held out her hand. "I'm almost through. Just four more stanzas."

"Sorry. I can't stanza anymore." I hid the music behind my back. "You know the rules."

She clucked her tongue. "I hate the rules."

"Rules are rules. You practiced this morning for at least an hour."

She bolted to her feet, grabbing at the music. I whipped it away. For a fat girl, I'm pretty quick.

She exhaled in disgust, then placed the clarinet in its case on the bed and sank down beside it. She drew her bony knees to her chest. "So, is dinner ready?"

"Yeah." I leaned against her full-length mirror. "If that's what you want to call it. Mom cooked."

"Again?" Vanessa curled a lip. "What is it this time? Tofu turkey?"

I smiled. "That actually sounds better than what she's making."

Van's eyes widened. "Maybe we could sue for cruel and unusual parents."

I laughed. She smirked. That was the sister I knew and loved. At the door I stopped and stared back at her.

"I'm coming," she said. Her eyes swelled out of their sunken sockets.

I closed the door, wondering, as I headed to my own room, whether my intervention was really helping Vanessa deal with her obsessive compulsive disorder. Dr. Sid, our psychologist, said it would. But then he chewed his nails until they bled. Who was helping him?

I wondered, too, if he was curing either of us of our real problem. No doubt he was writing us up in some medical journal: "From Out of the Same Gene Pool: Two Sisters—One Can't Eat; One Can't Stop."

Removing the package of Hostess cupcakes from the bottom of my underwear drawer, I breathed in their luscious aroma. My own eyes reflected back at me in the mirror. As if in conversation, one pair pleaded. The other beckoned. The first scolded.

"Ohhh . . ." I clucked. "All right." I shoved the cupcakes back under my bra, one cake per cup, and slammed the drawer. At least I wouldn't have to feel guilty for accidentally on purpose forgetting to write them down in my diary. Speaking of which, where was that empty diary?

Chapter 3

Lydia ambushed me the second I stepped off the school bus. "I found out Hugh's favorite color is brown," she said. "His lucky number is eight, and he loves anchovy pizza."

There was a pause, then, "Ewww," Lydia and I both gagged in unison.

I added, "What did you do, talk to him?"

"Are you nuts?" Lydia shifted her backpack to her other shoulder. "I asked Kevin Rooney."

My sandals stuck to the sidewalk. "Kevin Rooney?" Just hearing his name gave me gargantuan goose bumps.

Lydia twined her hair behind her ears and said, "Kevin is on Hugh's science team. I couldn't ask

Hugh—gawd forbid. Someone might see me talking to him. So I asked Kevin."

"How would Kevin know that Hugh likes anchovy pizza?" I asked. Kevin didn't speak a word of nerd.

Lydia exhaled an exasperated sigh. "He doesn't. I made up this fake survey." She handed me a sheet of paper. At the top, printed neatly in pink ink, was the title: *Sixth-Grade End-of-School Personal Interests Survey*. Below the title were the instructions: *Answer each question to the best of your ability.*

"This morning I asked Kevin to ask Hugh to fill it out," Lydia said. "I told him it was for a social studies project and that I needed it back right away."

My jaw unhinged. Lydia amazed me. She'd been busy. All I'd done last night was watch *Dawson's Creek*, devour a bag of barbecued potato chips while my parents were out cowboy boogying, and go to bed. "One question," I said. "Since when is Kevin on Hugh's science team? I thought he was on the tornado team."

Lydia clucked. "Where have you been? There were too many people on the tornado team, so Mr. Biekmund made them split up. Since Kevin's into computers, he asked him if he'd mind working with Hugh. Naturally Melanie went over with Kevin. She's sooo obvious." Lydia rolled her eyes.

"Tell me about it," I muttered.

"Ashley couldn't be left behind without her groupie, so she followed Melanie. Don't you remember the little snit she had? How she wanted to be in charge? How she hated Hugh's idea and wanted to do something else? You were there."

"Guess I was busy." Guess I was sleeping.

"Anyway," Lydia went on, "look at the last question."

I scanned down the survey and read aloud, "'Have you asked anyone to the spring fling?'" My eyes widened. "Lydia!"

She smiled. "He answered no."

"Kevin did?"

"No, Hugh." She gave me a funny look.

Hastily I hustled toward class. Lydia followed on my flopping heels. "So, did Kevin fill out a survey, too?" I said nonchalantly.

"I didn't ask him to," Lydia replied.

Rats. I'd give a month of Milk Duds to know his answer to the last question. To any of the questions. "Didn't Kevin wonder why you wanted Hugh to fill out the survey and not him?" My fingers curled around the door handle.

"Yeah, he wondered." As she passed by me on her way in, she smiled over her shoulder. "Let him wonder."

Oh, boy, was Lydia coy. About as coy as the brick wall she smacked into.

Eight. Brown. Anchovies. I wrote the words in my reading journal. I reread them. They sounded like the start of a poem.

> Eight brown anchovies
> On a pizza pie.
> I took one bite
> And thought that I would die.

Mrs. Jonas paused at my desk. She had her grade book open and, in her left hand, jiggled a red Flair pen. "Jenny, you have a spelling test to make up from last week and the daily oral language sentences to redo. Unless you want me to record the D plus." When I didn't reply right away, she arched both eyebrows.

"I'm thinking."

She pursed her lips. You know the look: That wasn't really a choice. Her wristwatch beeped, postponing my indecision. "Time for science," Mrs. Jonas announced to the class. "Mr. Biekmund asked me to remind you that your science fair project plans are due today."

Uh-oh, I thought. That's what we forgot to talk

about yesterday in the Peacemobile. I knew there was a reason we'd gotten together, other than delving into our deepest, darkest secrets.

Like a lumbering herd of buffalo, our class transferred to the science room. On the way Lydia had to say it: "We didn't talk about the project, Jenny."

"No duh," I said.

"What are we going to tell Mr. Biekmund?"

Max and Prairie looked at me, too. Sometimes being the leader is a major burden. "Leave it to me," I said. "I'll think of something."

Mr. Biekmund was his usual sniffly self. The Beak Man, we called him, because he had a nose like a garden hose. Terminal postnasal drip. He was always snuffling and blowing his snot out into a wadded-up handkerchief, too. Disgusting. You try to listen to a flat trombone for an hour every day — after an hour and a half of clarinet. No wonder I hated band instruments.

As soon as the dust settled, the Beak Man began picking up science fair plans. He couldn't wait until the end of class, could he? I mean, what's the rush? He hovered over our table, sniffing. "Ladies, do you have your project plans for the science fair?" he asked.

"Huh?" I said.

"Your science fair plans," he repeated.

I gave him my most shocked expression. "You mean now?"

"They're due today." His expression didn't change.

He was good, I had to give him that. "Um, well, to tell you the truth, Mr. Biekmund, my new puppy sort of had an accident on the plans."

"You have a new puppy?" Lydia piped up. "You didn't tell us. What's his name?"

I pummeled her with eye pellets. Max groaned.

"I'll have to give you all F's," the Beak Man said flatly. He started to saunter away.

"Wait," I called.

He stopped and swiveled back.

"Could I tell you about it, at least? I mean, I'm in the middle of recopying the plans, and I'll have them to you by the end of the day. You said due today, so I thought that meant by three-thirty. It wouldn't be fair to give everybody else an F just because my puppy peed on the plans."

He held my eyes.

I could feel the rest of the Squad arching pathetic eyebrows.

The Beak Man exhaled a long, weary breath.

I exhaled one myself. "Geez," I said, smiling, "I thought for a minute that you thought we didn't even *do* it." I gave a short laugh.

Max, Prairie, and Lydia laughed, too.

"So," the Beak Man said, "what's your project?"

"Our project." My mouth felt like I'd been sucking chalk. "Our project is . . ."

"An experiment," Max muttered.

"Right," I said. "An experiment. Like . . . how many M&M's are there in a bite-size bag as compared to the full pounder."

The Beak Man frowned.

"We're going to see if M&M's actually do melt in your hands, which everyone knows they do. Then we're going to sue M&M's for false advertising and make a million dollars for the school. To buy new science equipment, of course."

By his expression I could tell I'd exhausted the Beak Man's humor quotient. Which was zero to begin with.

"Just kidding," I said. "I'll have the plan to you by the end of the day."

After he left, the Squad gave me the thumbs-up. Sometimes school was like that. Dodge one disaster after another.

At lunch, after we'd settled at our table in the far corner, I said, "About the science fair—"

Lydia cut me off: "His favorite subject is math.

Well, computers really, and his favorite sport is bowling."

"Who?" I asked.

"Hugh."

"Who?" Max repeated.

"Hugh."

"Hugh's on first," I said. "What's on second. I don't know's on third." They stared at me like I had a dead cow on my head. "Never mind. One of my father's Abbott and Costello routines." It usually got the same response from Vanessa and me. So why had I repeated it?

Lydia reread the survey, shaking her head. "I don't know how we're going to use this information. Hmmm." She tapped her chin. The first part of Lydia's plan was to gather data on Hugh, since he was an unknown entity. I was coming to realize that people are unknown entities for a reason.

"What did Prairie say about the survey?" I asked.

Lydia replied, "I haven't shown it to her yet." A smile curled her lips. "She'll just die when she sees it."

"Or you will," Max muttered.

Lydia said, "Oh, good. Here she comes."

Prairie usually came to lunch a little later than us. After science she had special classes in the resource room, which we used to call the retard room before we knew Prairie.

"Hi, Prairie. Sit next to me." Lydia scootched over on the table bench to let Prairie slide in.

"I l-love spaghetti day." Prairie smiled. "D-don't you just love spaghetti day?" She wound a wad of day-old pasta around her fork and chomped into it.

While we ate, Lydia explained her plan and showed Prairie the survey. Prairie's eyes bugged out. She sucked in spaghetti while she sucked up Hugh's responses.

"If no one wants their brownie, I'll take it off your hands," I said. There was more pleading in my voice than I meant to betray. Slurping pasta, Prairie handed hers over. Max, even though she'd eaten half, surrendered hers. Lydia hesitated. Clucking her tongue, she added her brownie to the stack.

I smiled meekly. "I owe you one."

"Forget it," she said. "Although I feel like I should be helping you stay on your diet."

"It's not a diet. It's a nutrition plan. As long as I write down everything I eat, I can eat anything I want." That was my interpretation.

Lydia looked skeptical. "I guess your dietician figures if you're busy writing, you can't eat."

My fingers formed a fist to slug her. Max beat me to it. "Ouch." Lydia rubbed her arm. A blob of spaghetti sauce dribbled out of her mouth. Dabbing her lips with a napkin, she said, "Well, I should know. My mother's a—"

"Child psychologist," we finished for her. We heard this so often, we could recite it in a coma.

All of a sudden the air grew stale. A shadow enveloped us. "What's this I hear about a sixth-grade survey?" Ashley Krupps said. She loomed over Lydia, her bulk blocking what little light there was. Ashley was fat, like me. Only she didn't care. Next to Ashley stood Melanie. She flipped a spray of long blond hair over her shoulder. I tried that once in the mirror. Almost dislocated my sternum.

"It doesn't concern you," Lydia said.

Ashley replied, "You mean it's only for sixth-grade boys? That's discrimination."

Lydia clucked. "It's not just for boys."

Melanie flipped her hair again. "Then it must just be for Hugh. He's the only one who's mentioned it."

Ashley widened her eyes at Melanie, then narrowed them knowingly at Lydia. "So," she said, "someone's got the hots for Hugh."

Lydia sneered. "Get real."

"Get lost," Max mumbled.

Ashley turned to Melanie. "I guess I should tell them about Hugh asking me to the spring fling. I wasn't going to go, of course, but maybe now I will. Since you're going with Kevin. We could double."

Melanie smiled at me, like she knew my secret.

"Come on, I'm starving." Ashley waddled away. Melanie snitched a brownie off my tray and sashayed after Ashley. My body responded with sugar shock, or maybe just plain shock.

Prairie stared at Lydia, chin on chest.

"Don't believe her, Prairie," I said. "You saw the survey. Hugh said he hadn't asked anyone to the dance."

Prairie blinked at Lydia. "W-when did you give him the survey?"

"This morning," she said.

Prairie nodded slowly. I hoped she wasn't thinking what I was thinking. That between then and now some significant social event had transpired.

Prairie met my eyes, then looked away. Her lower lip trembled. "Excuse me," she said, sliding out. She walked away fast, leaving a half-eaten tray of spaghetti.

"I'm going to kill them," Max said, glaring across the cafeteria at Ashley and Melanie. It was no idle threat. "I'm going to cut off their—"

"Me!" Lydia said suddenly. "Ashley thinks *I* like Hugh?"

"Well," I said. "You *are* the one asking personal questions about him. And *only* him." Before Lydia could get her asthma up, I added, "Come on, guys. Let's go find Prairie. We'll kill the creeps later."

Chapter 4

Back in Mrs. Jonas's homeroom, I scribbled up a phony science fair plan ten minutes before the final bell. All I could think of was an enhanced M&M's experiment in which we'd also taste-test the different colors and rank them as to their deliciousness. Hey, it was late in the day. My blood sugar was low.

I rushed the plan over to Mr. Biekmund. Unfortunately he was there. Unfortunately he read the plan. Unfortunately he hated it.

I called an emergency meeting of the Snob Squad. Once we'd taken our places in the Peacemobile, I said, "We need to talk about the science fair—"

Lydia interrupted, "I know for a fact that Hugh

hasn't asked Ashley to the dance, Prairie. And Kevin hasn't asked Melanie, either. They're lying."

That erased the science fair from my agenda. "How do you know?" I said.

Lydia clucked. "Just because Ashley and Hugh and Melanie and Kevin are working on a computer project for the science fair, Ashley thinks they're all engaged. I know Hugh hasn't asked her to the dance. You know what a liar Ashley is. She just said that because she thought I was interested. Which I am *not*," she emphasized to Prairie's dark face.

Prairie didn't look convinced. Neither did I.

Then Lydia had to add, "But if Ashley really is after Hugh, then he's doomed. We better think of something fast."

Max said, "We could blow up the computer center."

"N-no," Prairie said. "If Hugh wants to ask Ashley, or anyone else, then he sh-should." She stared off across the van, into rust dust.

She was right. On the other hand, if Kevin wants to ask Melanie, or anyone else, maybe Max's plan was solid.

I didn't really want to, but the look on Prairie's face told me it was time to change the subject. "Hey, guys, we *have* to talk about the science fair. What are we going to do? The Beak Man didn't accept the M&M's

experiment." I passed around our after-school snack, a bag of peeled baby carrots that nobody would trade for at lunch. "He said he expected more." I rolled my eyes.

"I h-hate science," Prairie said.

Lydia sneezed. "I think I'm allergic to it."

Prairie exhaled a long sigh and added, "Why did Mr. Biekmund v-volunteer our class to represent the whole school?"

"Because he's transferring to Widener next year." Lydia crunched a carrot. "What does he care if Montrose Middle School comes in dead last in the whole district? What does he care if the entire student body is totally humiliated by our class's stupid science fair projects? It's no skin off his nose."

Mr. Biekmund was leaving? That was news to me. I sort of liked him, weirdo that he was. He didn't play favorites, not even with Ashley, the principal's daughter. And he really loved science—you could tell. Even though he rejected my plan, he didn't reject me. Know what I mean? It wasn't personal. It was a putrid plan. I admit it. "So what's our project going to be? I can't get an F in science, okay? I've already got one in social studies. And my language grade as of yesterday is a D plus. Come on, think."

There was communal crunching. "I've got it,"

Lydia said. "We could grow mold. That's always popular."

"Oh, yeah," Max muttered. "Especially in the cafeteria."

"My brother has m-mold growing in his car," Prairie said. "My d-dad says he gave him the perfect name: Yucca. Get it? Yuck? Car?"

Lydia said, "Your brother's name is Yucca? For real?"

Made sense to me. Prairie's last name was Cactus. "What are your other brothers' names?" I asked. She had six brothers. No wonder she was challenged.

Prairie counted on her fingers. "River, Sun, Moon, Forest, Mesa, and Yucca."

Prairie got teased mercilessly. I bet her brothers did, too. Parents who give their kids weird names should be shipped to Shanghai. Where is Shanghai, anyway?

Lydia said, "What's your Mom's name, Aloe Vera?" She hyena-howled.

Prairie replied flatly, "No. Her name is Marianne."

That shut Lydia up. Her mother's name was Marianne, too. Dr. Marianne Beals. How often did we hear that?

I sighed wearily. "People, people, people. The project?" God, I sounded like the Beak Man.

We all crunched in unison. The carrot bag made its way around. Prairie said, "Can we do an animal p-project? Last year my brother Sun h-hatched baby ducks in an incubator."

Max's eyes lit up. "How many?"

"Eight," Prairie said. "But one died."

"Aw." Max blinked away. She smiled tenderly. "I love baby animals."

We all stared at her. No one in their right mind would leave Max alone with a baby animal. I said, "I think by the end of sixth grade we're supposed to do more than watch eggs hatch. Now, if we could *clone* a duck . . ."

Lydia said, "Yeah, right. Who do you think we are, Einstein?" She paused and smiled. "Maybe we could clone Mr. Vance. You'd like that, wouldn't you, Jenny?" She wiggled eyebrows at me.

I zinged a carrot at her.

Max interrupted the ensuing food fight. "Could we train animals? Is that science?"

"Sounds like science to me," I said. "Does anyone have an animal?"

Lydia said, "You have a puppy."

I just looked at her.

"You don't have a puppy? But I thought . . . oh."

No one ever accused Lydia of being quick-witted.

"Last year I had Petey, my hamster," I said. "But, as you all know, he died on Halloween." Everyone lowered their heads in respect.

"Wait here." Max propelled herself to her feet and launched out of the minivan. Her army boots crunched gravel on the way to her house.

Lydia snapped a carrot in her teeth and said, "Maybe Max has a cloning kit." She grinned at me.

"Wouldn't surprise me," I said. Nothing Max did surprised me. I take that back. Everything Max did surprised me.

"C-could we b-borrow an animal?" Prairie said. "My cousin Butch has an iguana."

"I'm not touching any lizards," Lydia said. "They're infested with bacteria. Didn't you hear about those kids at the zoo who got food poisoning from touching the monitor lizard?" She shivered.

"Huh?" Prairie and I both frowned at her.

"They touched it, then they sucked their fingers," she explained.

"Why didn't they just b-buy a Popsicle?" Prairie asked.

I laughed. Lydia clucked. "Good one, Prairie," I said. "What could you teach a lizard? 'Hey, slimy. Roll over. Play dead. Pretend you touched a human and got food poisoning.'"

Prairie giggled. Even Lydia cracked a smile. Just then Max returned with . . . not a cloning kit. Something more interesting. A caged rat.

Lydia screamed.

"His name's Harley," Max said. " 'Cause I found him out by the Harley-Davidson parts. Here, Harley. Here, boy." She wiggled her index finger at him through the chicken wire. He sniffed it. "I bet we could train him. He's real smart. I saw on *Bill Nye, the Science Guy,* where these trained rats played basketball."

"You watch *Bill Nye, the Science Guy?*" Lydia widened her eyes at Max.

Max's eyes widened back. "Doesn't everyone?"

Prairie said, "N-not me. I hate science."

Max looked at me.

"It's on the same time as *Oprah.*"

"Horrors," Lydia mocked me. "You can't miss *Oprah.*"

I shot back at her, "What do you watch? *Barney?*"

Max snickered.

"No," Lydia mumbled.

"Then what?" I said.

"Nothing." Her cheeks turned pink. "I'm not allowed to watch TV."

"At all?" we intoned in unison.

Lydia's spine stiffened. "It's poison for the brain, my mother says. And she should know. She's —"

"A child psychologist," we all droned.

"Well, she is," Lydia said weakly.

"Bill Nye's not poison," Max replied. "He's educational."

"Same difference," I muttered.

Lydia snuck me a thank-you smile.

Leadership is such a trip. "Anyway," I sighed wearily, "getting back to the project, you think we could train Harley to play basketball, Max?"

"Nah," she said. "That's been done. We can teach him to play chess."

I laughed. We all laughed. Except Max.

"You're not serious," I said.

"Why not?"

"We only have three weeks," Lydia replied. "I'm not sure *I* could learn to play chess in three weeks."

"Then it's a good thing we're not trying to train you," Max said.

Lydia tensed.

"She's kidding, Lydia," I said. "But chess, Max? I don't know. Who are we going to find to play against him?"

"Yeah. Bugs Bunny?" Lydia crunched off a chunk of carrot and chomped noisily.

My palm intercepted Max's fist, which was headed toward Lydia's face.

Prairie said, "How about an obstacle c-course? We could b-build tunnels and m-mazes, stuff like that. At the end, Harley could r-ring a bell."

"Brilliant!" I cried. "What do you think, Max? Can we train Harley to run an obstacle course in three weeks?"

She studied the rat. With one hand she formed a tunnel over his head. "Hit it, Harley," she said.

In a flash Harley lunged through her hand to the other side. Watching him perch on his haunches to wash his whiskers, I thought, Who needs Bill Nye, the science guy, when you've got Maxine, the lean, mean, rodent machine?

Chapter 5

We had a family counseling session scheduled for Tuesday night. Dr. Sidhwa, our family psychologist, was pretty cool. Last month he'd helped me work through a major trauma in my life. Now he was working with Vanessa and playing marriage counselor for my parents. Dr. Sid, or as he pronounced it, Dr. Seed, had asked if we could all meet with him this week as a family unit. Family unit. No one in their right mind would call us that. Which made me wonder again about Dr. Sid.

When our clunky old station wagon pulled in next to Dr. Sid's parking space in the lot downtown, Dad muttered, "It's nice to know the Solanos are financing the good doctor's Ferrari."

Mom gave him the look. You know the one: Watch your language; there are children present.

We didn't speak the whole time it took to ride up in the elevator to the fourteenth floor. We were all nervous as gnats, I think. What would we say in front of one another, as a family unit? What could we say? Nothing close to the truth, for sure.

"Welcome, welcome. Glad to see you all," Dr. Sid greeted us. "Jenny, I'd like to talk to you alone first for a few minutes."

"Me?" I almost lost my black bean burrito. No big loss. "Sure, okay." I watched with panicked eyes as my family unit took seats in the waiting room.

"Have a chair." Dr. Sid motioned me into his office. He closed the door behind me. "How is your food diary coming?" he said. "I spoke with Minnette about it last week."

Minnette was my registered dietician. I wasn't sure what she was registered for; the Jenny Craig Lifetime Achievement Award, probably. She weighed about forty-five pounds—with her shoes on. "Fine," I said. "I mean, it's almost full."

He arched both eyebrows as if to say, "Already?" Instead he asked, "Have you discovered anything interesting about your eating habits?"

"Besides the fact that I eat all the time? Not really."
Dr. Sid smiled.

I added, "I do have a question. She said I should write down everything I eat. Does that include toothpaste? I mean, there must be calories in Crest, since it's so minty and sweet. Not that I'm eating toothpaste in globs or anything." I didn't add, Just that once when Mom made zucchini-and-bran biscuits for breakfast. I said, "If Mom asks where all the toothpaste is going, tell her it's Vanessa. You know how you're supposed to brush your teeth after every meal? Vanessa brushes her teeth after every bite."

Dr. Sid frowned.

"Not that she's worse," I said quickly. "She's a lot better. She hardly ever cuts her Cheerios in half anymore."

He smiled.

To myself I added, She just eats half as many.

"That's good to hear," he said. "And you're helping her by intervening when she starts to exhibit repetitive behaviors?"

"Yeah. I think it's working. I hope it is."

The conversation stalled. At least I'd managed to divert it away from me. Or so I thought.

"So," Dr. Sid said, folding his hands atop his desk.

"Have you identified certain times or situations when you feel a more powerful urge to eat?"

That was an interesting question. "As a matter of fact I have."

Dr. Sid arched an expectant eyebrow.

"Mealtimes," I said.

The eyebrow plunged.

"No, seriously. I remember how mealtimes used to be so much fun. We'd laugh and joke around, talk about all the stuff that was going on in our lives."

"And you don't do that anymore?" Dr. Sid said.

"No, we just . . . eat. At least I do. Vanessa moves food around on her plate. Nobody talks. It's tense."

He nodded, looking serious. Then he stood and said, "Thank you for telling me. That gives me some insight. Do you mind if I bring in everyone else now?"

"Uh, sure. You want me to leave?" I pushed to my feet.

He waved me back down. "Let's see if we can get this family talking again."

Dr. Sid ushered everyone in and asked them to sit. With one patient in there it was cramped. With four we'd be sitting on laps. I hoped I wouldn't get Dr. Sid's. In addition to his huge desk and big comfy chair, Dr. Sid had books and toys and electronic gadgets littered all over the place. Someone, his secretary probably, had carted in four folding chairs for our group. It was interesting, watching my family. They each grabbed a chair and retreated to the far corners of the room.

"So, how is everybody?" Dr. Sid folded his hands over his desk again and smiled.

In unison, as if we'd rehearsed on the way over, we chirped, "Fine."

Dad and I looked at each other and cracked up. Dr. Sid chuckled. Mom and Vanessa stared at the floor.

Dr. Sid said, "Okay. I'm going to go around and ask you each to say one good thing about your family. Something you appreciate or enjoy about one another."

Suddenly I understood the deeper meaning of dead silence.

"Katherine?"

Mom flinched. "I love my family," she said. "Why do you think *I'm* the problem? Did Jenny tell you something?"

A guttural sound of shock issued from my mouth.

"No," Dr. Sid said quickly. "Not at all. And I didn't say you had a problem. I just thought I'd start on the left."

"Oh," Mom mumbled. "Sorry."

Dr. Sid waited. When Mom didn't continue, he said, "I am certain that you love your family, Katherine. But could you be specific? What is it about them you love? Specifically?"

I interrupted, "Is this like Oprah's gratitude moment? You know, how you write down five things every day that you're grateful for and it's supposed to change your life?"

Everyone stared at me.

My face flared. "Never mind. Go ahead."

Dr. Sid smiled at me and focused back on Mom. "Katherine?"

Mom pursed her lips. "Everything. I can't pick just one thing. Are you saying there's something about my family I don't love? How can I be specific?"

Dr. Sid sighed and made a note on his yellow pad. Probably to go ahead and make that down payment on next year's Ferrari.

After we were done as a family unit, Dr. Sid asked to speak to Vanessa alone for a few minutes. She came out looking like she'd been crying. Mom and Dad looked concerned, but I guess they knew better than to ask. She'd snap their heads off.

The appointment ended pretty much the way it had started. We didn't speak the whole way home.

Chapter 6

As leader of the Snob Squad, it was my responsibility to get our science fair project off the ground. Duty can be a drag, except in this case. Thinking about the project gave my mind something else to dwell on besides the fact that (1) my family would be in long-term psychotherapy forever, (2) Melanie Mason had her claws in Kevin Rooney, and (3) I had to meet with Minnette, my nutrition Nazi, on Saturday to go over my food diary.

"Prairie and Max, you're in charge of building the obstacle course," I told them before school started.

"W-with w-what?" Prairie asked.

I knew she'd ask. "With whatever building supplies you can find around the house. Or, in Max's case, steal from the strip mall."

Max smirked at me.

"Lydia, you write down the daily observations of Harley's progress. Since you can spell."

She beamed. "And what are you going to do?" Lydia asked.

"Motivate the team, of course. Especially the rat." At the sound of his species, Harley peeked his head out of Max's jacket pocket. From my backpack I removed a limp carrot and dangled it over Harley's head. He snatched it out of my fingers faster than you can say, "Leggo my Eggo." Just as I suspected, Harley and I responded to the same stimulus—food.

I cornered Mr. Biekmund at his desk before science started and described our new and improved science fair project. "A trained rat?" he repeated. "I'm sorry, Jenny, but the science fair rules state no experiments with live animals."

"We're not experimenting," I told him. Although, I have to admit, dissecting Harley seemed more intriguing than watching him wiggle through milk cartons. "We're training him. We're demonstrating alternative learning styles. It's totally educational. We're not going to harm him in any way."

"Hmmm." The Beak Man sniffled. "I don't know."

"It's the only thing we could come up with," I

added. "Unless you want us to grow mold." Like how would that look for Montrose Middle School? Huh? Huh? You'd be the laughingstock of the entire scientific community. Good luck getting a job at Widener, or anywhere else. "Besides," I lied, "we already built the course."

He sighed. "All right. But I don't want you to bring a live rat to class."

"How 'bout a dead one?"

He didn't acknowledge the humor.

"You can work on your poster board display and type up your observations during science period."

We could continue zoning out, is what I heard. How was I going to tell Max not to bring Harley to school, since she'd already smuggled him in? He'd built a homey little nest in her camouflage jacket pocket. Maybe I'd accidentally on purpose forget to relay the Beak Man's message to Max.

Ashley and Melanie whooped with laughter over at the computer center, diverting Mr. Biekmund's attention and mine. "Oh, Hugh," I heard Ashley coo as she clenched his arm. "You are sooo smart." She glanced over her shoulder to make sure Lydia was listening.

Lydia heard all right. Prairie did, too.

Kevin said something, Melanie giggled, and I gagged.

A formidable force wrenched me backward. It was Lydia, tugging on my T-shirt. "I've got it," she said.

"Well, don't give it to me," I replied, lurching away.

"No, listen. I know how to break up that cozy little foursome. Max, come here." She waved her over.

Max blinked out of her usual reverie, staring across the crowded room, plotting some cerebral carnage. She clunked down off the heater vent, where she'd been perched, and lumbered over.

Lydia whispered, "Let's sabotage their project. Make it look like Ashley and Melanie wrecked it. That'll pit the guys against the girls."

"Yeah, right," I said. Melanie laughed again, and I added, "Okay, how?"

Max ambled away, but not before I caught the gleam in her eyes. She clomped across the room in her army boots and paused at the PC center.

"What's she doing?" Lydia asked.

"Don't ask me. Whatever you said hit a nerve. If I were you, I'd be nervous."

Max stuck a boot behind the first carrel and jerked. Without warning, all the computer screens went blank.

"Hey!" Ashley wailed. "What happened?"

Max twisted her head toward us. The most serene expression spread across her face.

Ashley hauled her extra-large carcass out of the chair and waddled around the carrel. When she saw the dangling plug near Max's boot, she almost shoved Max. Almost. Ashley wasn't stupid. Just stuck-up. And spoiled. She screamed, "Mr. Biekmund, tell Max to . . . to get away from here."

"Maxine?" the Beak Man warned.

Max cringed. She hated her name. Who didn't? "I tripped," she said.

Kevin groaned. He said, "We probably lost everything we keyed in today."

I felt sorry for Kevin. Even in despair, he was adorable. I personally would've rekeyed all his work, if he'd asked. Naturally he didn't. How can you ask someone something when you don't even know they're alive?

Ashley whined, "I'm not keying everything back in. You're the fastest typist, Hugh. You do it."

He stared at the blank screen, shook his head, and grumbled. "Well, move over then," he growled at Ashley.

Max smirked, spun on her boot heel, and sauntered away, snickering.

You gotta love her.

* * *

"The only way Hugh is going to notice Prairie is if she talks to him," Lydia announced at lunch. "She could bring up one of his favorite subjects, like how she just loves to bowl. And wouldn't it be fun to go bowling together sometime, hint, hint?"

I just looked at Lydia. Sometimes I wondered what her skull protected besides dead air. "She won't do it. She's too shy," I said. "Anyone want my asparaguts?"

Lydia spooned the slimy gray mass off my tray. "Maybe we could move her desk over by his," Lydia suggested. "Even though she's only in class for a couple of hours in the morning, he'd have to notice her sitting there."

"Don't count on it," I muttered. "His glasses are so smeared, he's lucky to see light."

"Okay," Lydia blabbered on, "then we put something of hers in his desk. Something he'd have to return."

"Like what?" I said. "Her fake foot?"

Max snorted.

Lydia gave me a dirty look. Swallowing a glob of green goo, she said, "We could change her looks. Do something drastic. Curl her hair, or dye it even."

"We could strap a PC on her back," I said. "He might notice that."

Lydia blinked at me. She didn't even smile. Her eyes stared past me, like Vanessa's used to do when she was totally obsessed. "Maybe we could somehow trick them into eating lunch at the same table. Order an anchovy pizza for him and say it was really Prairie's—"

Max made a retching sound. It stopped Lydia cold. "Please," Max said. "I'm trying to eat." She sucked in a slimy stalk of asparagus and swallowed.

I lost my appetite. For everything but the gingerbread, of course.

Lydia huffed. "Well, what are we going to do? We can't trust fate."

"We can't trust Ashley, you mean," I mumbled.

Max said something unintelligible through her asparagus.

"What?" Lydia snapped.

Max swallowed the glob. "I said, My brother's girlfriend works at Glamour Photos. She said I could come for a free sitting anytime. So I'm thinking, we'll send Prairie in my place. Then we stick her glamour photo in Hugh's desk and *voilà*."

"*Voilà*," I repeated. "Instant humiliation." I couldn't believe Max was suggesting this.

A slow smile curled Lydia's lips. "I love it!" she squealed. "Max, I love it!"

"Wait a minute," I said.

They high-fived. They held up their palms to me. When I hesitated, Lydia said, "What's the problem, Jenny? You act like you don't want to help Prairie."

"That's not true. I just think we should let her in on the plan. It's her life. Her love."

"And if she says no, which she probably will, then what? We give up? Is that what you want? To ruin Prairie's life?"

I glared at Lydia.

"Do you have a better idea?" she said.

I didn't. She knew it. She held up her palm. Max did, too. I had a bad feeling about this. A feeling of foreboding, like something was going to go terribly wrong. But what could I do? It was two against one. And I was their leader. The sound of my slap echoed across the cafeteria as Prairie said behind me, "W-what are we c-celebrating?"

Lydia scootched over to let Prairie in. "You and Hugh. A match made in heaven." She wiggled her eyebrows.

Prairie glanced across at me.

"We, uh, have a plan." I forced a grim grin. "You tell her, Lydia." I couldn't look Prairie in the eye.

Lydia huffed. "Oh, all right." She told Prairie about the plan, conveniently forgetting to mention the part about sneaking the picture to Hugh. I knew it was my responsibility to tell her, but Prairie seemed so excited about the glamour photo that I couldn't burst her bubble. Now could I?

Chapter 7

The Truly Amazing, Ultra-Impossible, Colossus Rat Contraption, aka the Extreme Rat-o-rama, began with a sheet of plywood that Max borrowed from behind the Ace hardware store. Borrowed, confiscated, swiped. We didn't ask, and she didn't tell. It was huge, dance floor size. Never mind getting the project off the ground. We'd barely got it in through the Peacemobile's door.

The first components of our obstacle course consisted of five one-gallon milk jugs, cut out on both ends; two Quaker oatmeal cartons, also cut out; a saltines box; and a rolling tower of TP tubes hot-glued together. Prairie said, "That's all I could f-find in our recycling b-bins."

Max contributed a jumble of car parts from the junkyard, including a steering wheel, a tire rim, an alternator (she called it), and a teeter-totter made out of two gas pedals welded together. She also threw in three stacks of Styrofoam and a hunk of foam rubber, which Harley was heartily devouring as we spoke.

"And last but not least," Max said, shoving her hand into a grocery bag, "ta-da." She pulled out a black box with buttons on it.

"What is it?" Lydia asked.

Max pressed the green button. The blare of a siren caused us all to scream and cover our ears. Max pressed the red button to turn it off. "It's an old ambulance siren," she said. "I had to bribe my brother to use it, so we better not bust it or anything. He'll make me lube chassis for a year."

"Geez, it's loud." I popped my eardrum back into place.

Max smiled. "I thought it'd be cool for Harley to set it off when he gets to the end of the obstacle course. Sort of like, 'Hey, everybody, I did it.' "

Lydia muttered in my good ear, "Let's hope he never makes it."

After Max duct-taped everything together, she positioned Harley at the start. He just stood there, looking panicked. "Here, Harley." Max snapped her fingers over the TP tower. "This way."

Harley's beady eyes bore into mine.

I seached my backpack. The only thing I could find was a package of crushed crackers with peanut butter. "Try this," I said.

Max ripped off a corner of the cellophane with her teeth, which unleashed a shower of cracker crumbs. She broke off a corner of cracker and held it over Harley's nose. He sniffed, then stood on his hind legs and wrapped his claws around Max's hand.

"He's going to bite you!" Lydia screeched.

Max gave her a withering look. Then Harley bit her.

"Yeow!" Max jerked back, sucking her bleeding thumb.

"Now you're going to get bubonic plague!" Lydia cried. "It comes from rats, you know. And it's highly contagious. You heard how a billion people died of the black death in Europe. Call 911."

Max rolled her eyes at me.

Really. I wondered, though, what is bluebonic plague? Was it related to Blue Bonnet butter? Did victims get a sudden craving for popcorn?

Prairie said, "Look, guys."

We all focused on what Prairie was pointing at. There, in the Extreme Rat-o-rama, Harley was wandering across the course, following the trail of cracker crumbs over all the car parts. I took the package from Max and smeared each rung of the steering wheel with peanut butter. Harley sniffed once, then one by one, tripped over each rung until he'd made a full circle. We all cheered.

"Lydia, quick," I said. "Get this down."

Lydia yanked out her science notebook. "I'm going to document the biting incident, too," she said. "Just in case."

As she scribbled, I scattered cracker crumbs into an oatmeal carton. Harley skittered through the carton, slurping them up. In a small voice, Prairie said, "I've b-been thinking about the plan."

We all turned to her.

I knew what she'd been thinking. Same thing I'd been. It was a stupid plan.

"I . . . l-love it." Prairie smiled.

My eyes grew wide as waffles. She must really have it bad for Hugh, I thought.

Prairie added, "I've always wanted to have a g-glamour photo. They make everyone look so b-beautiful. One thing I don't understand, though.

How is a g-glamour photo going to get Hugh to t-talk to me?"

See? my sneer said to Lydia. Did you think she was an idiot or something?

Lydia said, "We thought we'd stick the picture somewhere where Hugh would see it."

"Yeah, like in his pocket protector," I muttered.

Prairie's eyes bulged. "We c-can't do that at school. It's too risky. Why don't you let me t-take care of getting the p-picture to him?"

"Sure, okay," Lydia said. She sounded disappointed, as if she was now out of the running to be Prairie's maid of honor at the wedding.

Prairie said, "One m-more thing. I d-don't want to take a g-glamour photo alone. I'll only go if you guys c-come with me."

"Of course we'll come." Lydia wrapped an arm around Prairie's shoulders. "I've been dying to see how they take those pictures. How they turn really ugly pe —"

Max punched Lydia.

"Ow!" she yelped. Rubbing her arm, she said, "I mean, how they turn really ordinary people into supermodels. Not that you're ordinary, Prairie."

"No," I said, trying to salvage the situation. "You

actually have a brain." I made a face at Lydia, and she returned it.

Prairie shook her head. "I don't mean just come. I mean you have to have your p-pictures taken, too."

Lydia and I turned to Max. She stiffened. "All of us?"

Prairie smiled weakly and nodded.

Inwardly I warmed. A glamour photo? Me? The image of my face in the mirror, transformed from Jumbo Jenny into Supermodel Solano flashed through my brain. Then another thought streaked through. What if my gorgeous glamour photo somehow found its way into Kevin Rooney's possession? And what if he noticed me? Maybe this *was* a perfect plan. "All for one"—I held up my palm to high-five—"and one for all."

Chapter 8

I knew when I burst through the door at home that something was wrong. For one thing Vanessa wasn't practicing. She sat at the kitchen table, staring off into wall plaster. When she saw me, she blinked and pressed a finger to her lips.

"What?"

Then I heard it. Or felt it. Charged linoleum, powered by the bellowing from the basement. "I thought we agreed to do this together," my mother's angry voice streamed up the stairs. "I thought we were going to find something in common to do together."

A clunk against the basement wall made both Vanessa and me jump. My father said, "I hate dancing. I've always hated dancing. You know that."

Ominous footsteps pounded on the stairs. Like a

scared pig, I skittered off to my room, where those Hostess cupcakes beckoned from the dresser drawer. Maybe I'd even write them down.

I took out my food diary and flipped to an empty page. It happened to be page two. Rather than jotting down *Cupcakes, Hostess, both of them,* I wrote, *Jennifer Marie Rooney.* It had a nice ring.

Jenny Rooney. Very nice.

Mrs. Kevin Rooney. The ring went flat.

Mom never used *Mrs. Robert Solano.* In fact, I'd never seen her write *Mrs.* Just *Katherine T. Solano.*

Maybe that was her problem. She wasn't a Mrs. What was a Mrs. anyway? A name? A title? A wife for a Mr.? A mother of misses? Not that the problems she and Dad were having were all Mom's fault. I didn't know whose fault they were. Probably Vanessa's. Her multitudinous disorders had brought my parents to the brink. And my overeating had pushed them over.

Mrs. Jennifer Marie Rooney. Yes.

I sighed. It sounded so romantic. That was it! That's what was wrong. Mom and Dad weren't romantic. About the same time we lost our dinner discussions, Mom and Dad had lost their romance. It used to embarrass me, the way they'd hug and kiss in the kitchen. I was glad when it stopped. Except now I wasn't so glad. Something had changed between them. Something major. But what?

A knock on my door made me slap my food diary closed and slide it under the covers. "Yeah?"

Vanessa opened the door. "Dinnertime," she said. "Mom made liver linguine." She stuck an index finger in her mouth. "Needless to say, Dad went out."

Yes, the romance was definitely dead.

"My brother's girlfriend says she'll take our glamour photos," Max informed us at lunch the next day. "On one condition."

We all stopped chewing and stared at Max. She guzzled down her third carton of chocolate milk. It gave us time to swallow, too.

"Well, what is it?" Lydia asked.

"My brother has to propose to her."

"You mean, marriage?"

Max nodded.

My eyes bugged out. Scuzz-Gut? Someone actually wanted to marry Scuzz-Gut? He was such a freaky guy. Grungy, too. Plus he drank beer like it was Kool-Aid. Made me shudder to imagine what his girl-friend was like. "What's her name?" I asked Max.

"Caressa," she said.

"Scuzz-Gut and Caressa." I shook my head. Sounded like an Oprah show to me. "So when's the wedding?"

"Ain't gonna be no wedding." Max fed Harley a hunk of her sandwich crust. "My brother isn't ready for marriage."

"What's to be ready for?" I replied. "You say, 'I do,' and live happily ever after. . . . On second thought," I added, "maybe he shouldn't rush into anything."

"If he's not ready, he definitely should not get married," Lydia said. Spoken like the child of a child psychologist. "My parents got married too soon, and it didn't work out."

That was news to me. We'd never actually talked about Lydia's father. Just assumed she had one. Most people do. "Why'd they get married too soon?" I asked.

Lydia's face turned red as rhubarb.

"Oh," I muttered. "Never mind."

Prairie patted Lydia on the back. "It h-happens. My aunt B-Bethany had to get married."

Max said, "So, unless we can come up with two hundred and fifty dollars for the shoot, we're outta luck."

"Two hundred and fifty dollars? Forget it," I said. "If I had two hundred and fifty dollars, I'd buy a McDonald's franchise."

We all chewed for a moment in silence. Then Lydia piped up, "Prairie could still have hers done, right? You said Caressa offered you a free session. We'd be there; we just wouldn't get glamourized."

"Actually—" Max choked on her sandwich. She shoved the rest of it into her pocket for Harley and continued, "Caressa said the free offer was only for me. Not my friends. Because she has ulterior motives." Max's eyes dropped like lead.

"Oh," Lydia said.

We all sighed wistfully.

"M-maybe we could t-take our own glamour photos," Prairie said slowly. "My b-brother Moon got a new camera for Christmas. I b-bet he'd let me b-borrow it."

Lydia lit up. "That's a good idea. I have a bunch of dress-up clothes from when my mom was a showgirl in Las Vegas."

We all stared at Lydia. I said what we were thinking, "Your mother, the child psychologist, was a stripper in Vegas?"

Lydia scoffed. "Not a stripper. A performing artist.

Before she became a child psychologist. That's how she worked her way through college. Didn't your parents work their way through college?"

"Yeah," I said. "My dad did a double shift at Denny's. But I think he threw away the uniform."

Max snorted.

Lydia went on, "Why don't I ask my mom if you guys can sleep over? Then we can take our glamour photos. I can't do it this Saturday because I have a ballet recital. But maybe the next weekend. As long as we don't eat in the living room or watch TV, it'll probably be okay."

"We can eat in the kitchen, can't we?"

Over her glasses, Lydia narrowed her eyes at me. "Just checking."

We spent our after-school social hour the rest of the week putting Harley through his paces. He was getting closer to the ambulance siren every day. He was also getting fatter by the obstacle.

"Are you sure Harley is a he?" I asked Max on Friday. "Are you sure you shouldn't have named him Harlena?" We watched the fat rat scrabble over a car radio and squeeze through a milk jug. He used to wriggle through the jug a whole lot easier. I added,

"We might be looking at a litter of little Harleys by tomorrow."

"No way," Max said. She clucked. But she lifted Harley and studied his underbelly.

"If he does have babies, they better come after the science fair," Lydia said. "I refuse to document the live birth of baby rats." She shuddered.

"I don't know," I thought out loud. "We might get extra credit. In fact, maybe we should build one long tunnel. Harley starts at one end and by the time he reaches the other, there are eight Harleys. We claim cloning!"

Everyone laughed. Prairie said, "C-can I name one of the babies Hugh?"

"You can name all the babies Hugh," I said to her. To myself I added, Except the one I'm calling Kevin.

"Ain't gonna be no babies," Max said. "Except those Baby Ruth bars. Pass 'em over, Solano."

I opened the six-pack that we'd bought at 7-Eleven on the way over and tossed her one, all the while watching Harley/Harlena, and wondering if he or she had found a little rat romance out in the wreckage.

Chapter 9

Minnette bounced into the waiting room, the glow of good health illuminating her aura. "Hey, Jenny. Hey, Mr. Solano," she greeted us. Even her teeth were gleaming. "Sorry I'm late. Whoo, sure is hot today." She swiped her brow with a wristband.

I muttered to Dad, "What, did she ride her Exercycle over?"

He ignored me, he was so intent on reading the recipes in *Redbook*. Sometimes I wondered about Dad.

"Come on in, Jenny," she said. "This shouldn't take long."

Long is relative, I thought. The ten minutes I'd been sitting here had churned up a major stomachache.

Dad set the magazine back on the stack and stood. "I'm going down to the cafeteria for some coff—uh, some juice and a bran muffin."

Right, I thought. Sludge and a sugar doughnut is more like it.

"So, Jen." Minnette hopped up on the desk and motioned me to a chair. "How's the food diary coming?"

Call me Jen one more time, I seethed inwardly, and I'm outta here. We're not bosom buds. Okay, Min? She was so perky. So jerky.

She waited.

I shrugged.

"So"—she stuck out a hand—"let's see it."

I exhaled wearily. For appearance's sake, I rummaged through my backpack. "Wow." My voice was flat as her chest. "I guess I lost it."

Minnette pursed her pink lips. Her eyes met mine.

I vegged.

She jumped off the desk and dropped into the chair next to mine. "You didn't do it, did you?"

I clucked. How'd she know?

"Want to know how I know?" she asked.

Geez. She was skinny and psychic, too. Life isn't fair.

"Because I didn't do mine the first time, either. Oh,

maybe I filled in a day or two, then thought, This is a joke. A food diary? How's that going to make me stop eating? So I turned it into a joke. I wrote, *Dear Mrs. Butterworth, Today I ate a double stack of pancakes —with extra syrup. Yummee.*"

It made me look over at her. "How come you had to keep a food diary?"

She blinked. "Because I used to be fat. Very fat."

That surprised me. "How fat?"

"Two hundred and sixty-nine pounds."

My eyeballs swelled. Fatter than Oprah at her peak.

"Wow!"

"Yeah, wow," Minnette said. "We're talking obese. I lost it, but it was a struggle. Sometimes I still get the urge to eat a whole cherry cheesecake, all in one sitting."

I might have smiled. "Maybe you should see a registered dietician about that."

Minnette laughed. "I do. And I keep a food diary. It helps me keep track of how I'm doing. Especially during the tough times."

My eyes slid down to study her petite feet. "What if all the times are tough?" I asked.

She reached over and squeezed my knee. "They are, in the beginning. But once you change your habits . . ." Minnette let go and leaned back in her seat. "I don't need to tell you this stuff, Jenny. You know what it takes to lose weight."

"Yeah, eat right and exercise." I rolled my eyes.

"No!" She lunged at me. "It takes a passion. A need. A desire to change. A burning desire. Right here." She jabbed a fist in my middle.

My stomach muscles clenched. The only thing I had a burning desire for right now was a big fat jelly doughnut.

Minnette stood up. She grabbed a stack of folders off the desk and bounded toward the door. "I'd like to see you again, Jenny, but I won't make an appointment. It's Dr. Sid's feeling that this is something you want. I'm here for help and support. But I can't do this for you. Neither can Dr. Sid, or your parents, or anyone else. You have to do this for yourself." She opened the door. "So, call me when you're ready."

She left me there alone. All alone. And miserable. In the glass of the framed diploma on the opposite wall, my reflection blinked back. A tear slid down my cheek. You're a real glamour puss, the reflection said.

"Shut up," I shot back. "And show me where the Kleenex is."

Chapter 10

They called themselves the Cyber Stars. Ashley, Melanie, and our two true loves. Two of them were stars. The other two were black holes in cyberspace. Ashley had this thing about always coming up with a team name. She said it promoted teamwork. Baloney. She just wanted to pass on the blame to her teammates if anything went wrong.

On Monday Lydia, Max, Prairie, and I sort of moseyed over to the PC's to sort of spy on the Cyber Stars. Discreet like.

"Mr. Biekmund, the Blob Squad is spying on us," Ashley hollered across the room.

"That's Snob Squad to you," Lydia said.

"Huh?" Ashley cupped an ear. "The Slob Squad?"

Max raised a fist to silence Ashley forever, but I held her back. We didn't need to get busted for breaking Ashley's braces or anything. Ashley could get us suspended just for invading her space.

"Why aren't you girls working on your project?" Mr. Biekmund said.

I answered, "Because you won't let us bring the ra—uh, the project to school. And we already finished the write-up. Right, Lydia?"

"Uh, right," she lied. "As much as we have. So we wanted to play computer games. But the *Cyborg Stars*," she said in a singsong, "are always hogging the PC's." Lydia sneered at Ashley.

Melanie turned around. "We need both of the computers, Mr. Biekmund. Part of our project is networking the two machines together. Right, Kevin?"

"Yeah," he mumbled. "It's a communications project." He looked right at me. Or through me, though I didn't know how that was possible.

I swooned anyway. Hook *all* the computers together, I thought. I'll drag them over to your house.

The Beak Man pulled out his rank hankie. "I don't think playing computer games is appropriate while everyone else is working on their projects. Do you?"

We just stared at him dumbly.

Lydia was about to protest when the air grew

odiferous. I knew that stench. Everyone at school knew that stench and what followed it. Mr. Krupps's Old Spice and him, in that order. "Good afternoon, Mr. Biekmund. Class." He faked a smile.

Everyone dummied up.

"How are we coming along with our science fair entries?"

"Fine. Great," Mr. Biekmund answered. He slid us a sidelong glance, the classic evil eye, and we shuffled back to our desks to act busy.

"I thought I'd come by and have a look-see."

Behind me I heard Ashley moan. Even though she was the principal's daughter (and used her position to full unfair advantage), there were times I know she hated it. I mean, I would. Always having your father around, spying on you?

Mr. Krupps stopped at the first table and asked to see their project. "Oh, great," Lydia muttered beside me. "What are we going to show him?"

"Your notebook," I said. "That's all we've got."

"Not quite." Max lifted Harley out of her pocket.

Lydia scootched around in front of Max. "Put him back," she whispered loudly. "If Mr. Krupps sees him, he'll burst a blood vessel. You know we can't bring live animals to school."

"Maybe we could teach him to play possum," I

suggested. Unfortunately, Prairie's titter caught Krupps's attention. He meandered over.

"Let's see your science project, Ms. McFarland." He met Max's eyes. We all hated how he singled her out.

I said, "Show him your notebook, Lydia."

She reached into her bookbag and pulled out the notebook. As she handed it to Mr. Krupps, I noticed that sometime since yesterday she'd painted a title on the cover in puffy paint. *The Extreme Rat-o-rama*, I think it said. The paint was so thick, it blobbed.

Mr. Krupps read the first page. He eyed Max again. "This is fine, but where's *your* project, Ms. McFarland?"

I answered for her, "It's our project." I indicated the four of us. "We're a team."

Mr. Krupps set Lydia's notebook down on the table. "Looks like Lydia's doing all the work."

That made me mad. "No, she's not." Thinking fast, I dug in my backpack for my language notebook. "We're all keeping notes. See?"

He took the notebook from me.

I freaked. I didn't think he'd actually take it. Worse than that, what I'd grabbed was my food diary. Before I could even peep a protest, he flipped the cover open.

He frowned. "I don't understand. What is this project? Something about rats? And food?" He turned the page.

My heart stopped. If he read page two out loud, I'd have to kill myself. Fortunately Prairie piped up, "It's an obstacle c-course." In a smaller voice, she added, "For a r-rat."

"A rat?" he bellowed. Dropping my diary on the table, he scanned the room with his beady eyes. "Mr. Biekmund?"

Surreptitiously, I slid over to snatch up my diary, but I couldn't get to it through the crowd that had gathered. Some days I'd sacrifice my sister to be skinny.

Mr. Krupps located our science teacher, hiding behind Hugh in the back of the mob. "I didn't think animal projects were allowed."

"In this case"—the Beak Man stepped out and smiled wanly—"I gave special permission. It's a special project."

"Tell me about it." Mr. Krupps grinned at Max. It wasn't a friendly grin. More like, This better be good.

Lydia said, "We're creating a closed learning environment to test the—"

"I want to hear from Ms. McFarland," Krupps cut Lydia off. He zeroed in on Max.

Ashley, whose bulk was blocking me from getting my diary, said, "Yes, Max. Tell us *all* about it."

Max's eyes darted around. Without warning, without thinking, she whipped Harley out of her pocket and plopped him on the table. Several shrieks burst eardrums, and the crowd lurched back.

All except Mr. Krupps. He looked horrified.

I tried to intervene. "Our science project is called the Extreme Rat-o-rama. We're training this rat to run an obstacle course. It's, uh, real scientific."

"Scientific?" Mr. Krupps's raised voice hit a new high.

"It is!" Lydia leaped in. "Harley is a certified laboratory rat. An experimental specimen who will master an almost impossible task. He will complete, in sixty seconds or less, the world's toughest obstacle course. In other words, we're going to demonstrate the intelligence of lower life-forms."

"Oh, brother." Ashley snorted beside me.

Lydia, I thought, you win the Cracker Jack surprise.

Krupps's narrowed eyes spelled skeptical.

Lydia babbled on, "We're recording all of our observations. Every task Harley masters. That way the project will be preserved on record for future scientific study."

"Cool," Kevin said behind her.

"Very," Hugh put in.

Sometimes diarrhea of the mouth is Lydia's best quality. I wondered what Kevin would do if I leaped over the table and kissed him. Never mind. It was enough to hear him speak.

Mr. Krupps pursed his lips. "It is interesting," he said. "But—"

"But you're right," I joined in. "We have a problem." Before he could confiscate Harley or suspend Max, I said, "Since we're not allowed to bring live animals to school, we can't work on our project here." Mimicking Lydia's brownnose nasal whine, I added, "We may not get it done in time for the science fair." I proferred my most pathetic look.

Lydia caught my cue. She could do pathetic better than anyone I knew. Wait a minute. Prairie's pathos outpaced Lydia's by miles. Max only had the one look. Threatening.

"Well," Mr. Krupps considered. At that moment Harley scrabbled over to Mr. Krupps and started sniffing. Apparently the aroma of Old Spice was an aphrodisiac to rats, because Harley closed his eyes and swooned. Mr. Krupps smiled. A genuine smile. Maybe the first one ever. He reached down and scratched Harley's head. Harley let out a little whimper before spreading out all four legs and sprawling across the tabletop. Everyone went, "Awwww."

Mr. Krupps laughed. "All right," he said. "I'll make an exception. In this one instance, and only until the science fair. You are allowed to bring the rat to school."

"Yay!" we cheered. Max high-fived us.

"But," Krupps added, "I want him caged unless you're working with him. I won't have a rat running around free in Montrose Middle School. Now, Ashley, let's see this phenomenal technological wonder you've been bragging about at home for a week."

Ashley's fat face froze. She whirled, but not before Lydia got in a good jab. "Suck-up," she sniped.

Ashley waddled away.

Suddenly we heard a voice behind us. "What's the obstacle course like?"

We all held our breath. It was Hugh. And he was talking to Prairie.

She paled. "Y-y-y . . . y-y-y—"

"You'll see," I saved her. "Tomorrow. We'll bring it in."

Hugh turned and smiled at me. "I can't wait."

Chapter 11

Lydia tossed her backpack on the Peacemobile's sofa and said, "It's all set for Saturday night. My mom says she'll need to call your parents first, but you can all sleep over. She'll even help us with our hair and makeup."

I'd never actually seen Lydia's mom, but if she looked anything like Lydia, I didn't think we'd want her helping us with our hair and makeup.

"We n-need to finish the obstacle c-course today," Prairie said. "So it'll look good for tomorrow."

"You mean so Hugh will be impressed," Lydia said.

Prairie blushed. "He actually t-talked to me." She sighed. But only a short sigh before sobering. "Max," she ordered, "hand me that d-duct tape."

I got out the SnackWells granola bars and took my

usual two. A blurred vision of my nutrition Nazi flashed through my brain, and I reluctantly put one back. While the box went around, Lydia scrounged in her bookbag. "That's weird," she said. "I can't find my science notebook. I got it out to show Mr. Krupps. I thought I put it back."

My breath caught. Did I have my food diary? I plowed through my pack. Yes. Oxygen flowed again. There it was, right on top.

"Hey, g-guys. Something's wrong with Harley."

We all dashed over to the Rat-o-rama. "You're right," I said. "He doesn't look so good."

"He's fine," Max replied. "He's just tired from all the excitement."

Harley seemed beyond sleepy to me. More like comatose. Max tempted him with a corner of granola bar, and he sprang to life. "See?" she said. She trailed crumbs over the obstacle course while Harley scrabbled after them. About halfway across, though, where he's supposed to run through the oatmeal box, Harley stopped and sprawled flat on his belly. He was breathing hard.

I looked at Max.

"He's pooped," she said. "Give him a break."

"There," Prairie said. "I think the c-course is c-complete."

"I think Max is going into labor," I said. "He—she could deliver anytime."

"Damn!"

We all turned to Lydia, wide-eyed.

"Sorry," she mumbled. "I can't find my notebook. And it had all my notes about Hugh in it, too."

"Hugh?" Prairie perked up. "You m-mean the survey?"

Lydia nodded. "Plus a, uh, couple of ideas about getting you two together that I jotted down. Where *is* it?"

"Don't get your asthma up," I said. "You probably just left it in the science room. Anyway, there isn't anything new to write." Yet. No babies had popped out. "Harley hasn't made any progress at all. Maybe I'd better start bringing some real food. Like Hostess cupcakes, or Ding Dongs. Hey, Harl," I said to him, "would you ring the bell for a Ding Dong?"

That cracked everyone up.

I added, "Think I'll pick up a family box. Looks like Harley may be eating for more than one."

Dinner that night was meat loaf and mashed potatoes. Mr. Mom's specialty. Mrs. Mom added a can of peas to round out the meal. It was better than spaghetti and wheatballs, but not much. What was worse, there was no dessert. Worse than worse, if there is such a thing, no one talked through the whole meal. Forget rekindling the romance. Since their fight in the basement, Mom and Dad seemed to repel each other like opposite poles of a magnet. The peas repelled me. And Vanessa counted each chew of meat loaf to herself. God, she was obsessed about her weight. Unlike me, who emptied the bottle of ketchup over my meat loaf and swirled half a stick of butter into the potatoes to make a lava melt.

"When's our next therapy session?" I said, shattering the silence. They all stared at me. "You know, help for the helpless? Hope for the hopeless? Do I have to spell it out? D-i-s-f-u-n-k-s-h-o-n... whatever."

Mom got up to clear the table. "We are not dysfunctional," she said. "Who told you that? We're a perfectly normal family."

My eyes met Vanessa's. She was thinking what I was. This is normal?

"Your father and I have a marr—a separate counseling session next Monday, but it doesn't concern you." Mom whirled on Dad. "You see? Now our children think we're dysfunctional." She slammed the lid on the dishwasher and stormed out.

Dad looked at Vanessa, then me.

"Dad, I—"

"Just eat your meat loaf," he cut me off.

Vanessa scootched back her chair.

Dad said, "Where are you going?"

She replied, "To my room. I'm not hungry."

"Come back here!"

Her door slammed.

Dad sighed, and I forced a smile. "Guess that leaves you and me to clean up," I said. "Did I ever tell you how much I love your meat loaf?" I sawed through the hunk on my plate, which wasn't easy since it had the consistency of cardboard, then popped it in my mouth, swallowed it whole, and added, "An Arby's Jamocha shake would sure go good with it."

He didn't take the hint. Just started smashing peas under his fork.

"Ever see that bumper sticker, *Imagine Whirled Peas?*" I asked him.

He blinked up at me, eyes vacant.

"Never mind," I muttered.

From my school bus's back window, I spotted the car immediately. It was a distinctive automobile. A rebuilt Chevy Camaro. Body by Rust-Oleum. Engine by Joe Camel. Max slammed the trunk while Scuzz-

Gut unbent his beer belly enough to reveal . . . what? An armload of something draped in black silk. Of course. The Extreme Rat-o-rama. The black silk tablecloth must've been borrowed from Max's mom, Sibylique. She was a channeler. You know, a fortuneteller? A link to the spirit world? It embarrassed Max no end. I thought it was cool.

"Yo, Max," I called to her as I stepped off the bus. She nodded acknowledgment while I bustled over to them. A bigger, better cage for Harley, constructed out of screen and wood, swung from Max's hand.

"How far do we have to go?" Scuzz-Gut grumbled. "This damn thing's heavy."

"To the temps." I pointed to the mobile units across the baseball field. "Unit C."

"Ship," he muttered. Or something like that. He reeked of beer. Must've poured it over his Rice Krispies this morning. Snap, crackle, foam.

"Is that it? Is that the Extreme Rat-o-rama?" Several people gathered around. I guess everyone in school had heard about our science project. Nothing like live animal experiments to roust the roadkill. In the rear of the crowd, Hugh loomed large. Kevin hovered at his wing tips.

"Keep back," I said. "It's very, very fragile."

Max looked at me. So it was held together with six

rolls of duct tape. So a demolition derby couldn't destroy it.

"And don't touch the rat," Max warned. "He could have rabies."

"Or babies," I muttered.

"Can we see him?" someone asked.

"No," Max replied, hiding Harley behind me. "Get lost."

I added, "Harley, the wonder rat, will be making his debut today at nine-thirty, Science Lab One."

"The wonder rat?" Melanie scoffed. She moved up real close beside Kevin. Too close. Even I could smell her Powder Fresh Arrid Extra Dry. "Oh, brother," she said, sort of leaning into him.

He looked at me and smiled. I must've been hallucinating from Mom's attempt at breakfast: fennel fritters. "Should be exciting," Kevin said.

"You don't know what exciting is." I wiped the drool off my chin.

Chapter 12

All morning long people tried to sneak a peek at the Extreme Rat-o-rama. Or at Harley, the wonder rat. A steady stream of lookie-loos wandered by Max's desk in back, as everyone took the long route to the pencil sharpener or the drinking fountain. Lydia and I switched off guarding the project, since Max was busy with Harley. After my neck developed a permanent crick from twisting around so often, I asked Mrs. Jonas if we could all just move our desks to the back. "To keep Harley from escaping," I told her. "He's extremely intelligent, you know."

"By all means," she said. She was making an obvious effort to stay as far away from our rat as possible.

Right before science, Ashley and Melanie meandered by to harass us. "The Extreme Rat-o-rama." Ashley clucked. "I'm sure. I bet it's just a bunch of junk car parts all taped together. And Harley is a junk-yard rat. 'Certified laboratory rat.' Gimme a break."

"Name the bone," Max snarled. She held up a fist. Ashley lurched back.

We all sneered.

Ashley and Melanie rolled their eyes and sashayed off to sharpen their glitter pencils.

"How'd she know where we found Harley?" I whispered to Lydia. "And what the Rat-o-rama really is?"

Lydia's teeth ground together. Then her jaw unhinged. "She stole my notebook!" Her eyes narrowed. "Ashley stole my notebook. Now she knows all our science secrets."

Science secrets? What was Lydia writing in there?

"Worse than that, she has my notes on Hugh."

That was bad. Bad for Prairie.

"Guess we'll just have to steal it back," Max said.

Like a firing squad, we took aim with our eyes at Ashley's broad backside. "We'll do it at lunch," I whispered, "when they're out of the room."

"Let's go, people." Mrs. Jonas stood, checking her watch. "Everyone in line for lab."

For the first time ever, people actually hustled to line up for science. They couldn't wait to see our project. Hugh and Kevin paused by our desks. "Can I help you carry that thing?" Hugh asked.

"No, we've got it." Lydia hefted up a corner.

I elbowed her hard.

"Oh." She stumbled backward. "You can carry this side."

Hugh grabbed the corner, which happened to be next to Prairie's. Her freckles sizzled. No kidding— you could hear them.

"Here," Kevin said. "I'll take this edge." His hand brushed across mine as he grasped my corner. The tingle up and down my arm lasted all the way to the science wing.

The Rat-o-rama Revealed was an unforgettable event. At least I'll never forget it. Lydia, Prairie, and I performed a finger drumroll on the science sink while Max lifted the black silk tablecloth. Everyone gasped. Right before they burst into laughter.

"See?" Ashley squealed. "It's just a bunch of junk."

The whole class shook their heads and wandered back to their own projects. Except Hugh and Kevin. "So, how does it work?" Hugh asked.

Max retrieved Harley from his cage, where he was

deep in rat dreamland, and plopped him down at the start. I set a Gummy Worm at one end of a gallon milk jug. Harley sort of quivered in place, then yawned, wiggled his nostrils, and scurried through the carton. He snarfed the worm in one slurp. I continued the trail of Gummy Worms over tubes, through cartons, and around the steering wheel. At which point Harley stopped. He was breathing hard. Suddenly he sprawled in place and fell asleep.

"Wow," Hugh and Kevin said together. Kevin added, "Pretty neat."

"Hugh, Kev, come on!" Ashley shrieked from the PC center.

They jumped. Before leaving, Hugh reached down and scratched Harley's head. "What happens at the end?" he said, speaking to Prairie.

She froze in shock.

I smiled coyly. "It's a surprise."

Hugh smiled back at me. His eyebrows wiggled. "I like surprises."

After he lumbered off, Prairie grabbed my arm. "Did you h-hear that? Hugh l-likes surprises."

"If he likes surprises, we'll give him a big one," Lydia said. "After he sees your glamour photos, he won't be able to keep his eyes off you."

Prairie beamed. She looked so happy, I thought she might pop right out of her prosthesis.

Back in homeroom after science, Mrs. Jonas told us to line up for lunch. Lydia, Max, and I stalled around. "Girls, we're waiting." Mrs. Jonas cocked her head.

Max said, "We'll catch up. We gotta feed Harley first."

Lydia added, "Since we all brought our lunches today, could we eat here, Mrs. Jonas? We don't feel right about leaving Harley alone."

"Don't worry," Mrs. Jonas said. "I'll lock up."

I said, "What if he gets out while we're gone? What if he chews up a library book?"

Mrs. Jonas flinched. The consequence of returning mutilated materials to the media center . . . well, it was too hideous to imagine.

"Okay," she relented. "I assume I can trust you girls to clean up your mess."

We all gave her our "totally insulted" look.

"Tell them to keep out of our stuff," Ashley said behind her.

"Ashley, really." Mrs. Jonas frowned.

We copied the frown and added a sneer to bolster its effect.

As soon as everyone was gone, we ransacked Ashley's desk, looking for Lydia's notebook. "It's not here," Lydia wailed.

"Let's try Melanie's desk," I said.

No luck there either. But she did have a tube of blue eye shadow that I pocketed. Then immediately felt guilty about and lobbed back in.

Max said, "What about the guys? Hugh and that Rooney Tunes geek?"

I shot her a dirty look. Hearing my true love trashed was not to be tolerated.

Lydia started toward Hugh's desk.

"You better not let Prairie find out that you think Hugh might've taken it," I said.

The door flew open, and Prairie plodded in. "Hugh might've t-taken what?"

Our eyes darted around. "That's who," I said. "I mean, you. Taking you. Hugh is taking you to the dance. And we're so jealous, we could spit."

"Yeah, r-right." Prairie flung her pack over her desk chair and added, "You d-didn't tell me we were eating in the classroom. I had to ask M-Mrs. Jonas where you guys were."

"I was just coming down to the cafeteria to find you," I lied. Max dropped a book behind me, and I scootched over in front of Hugh's desk to hide her handiwork.

"What are you doing in Hugh's desk?" Prairie asked.

Was I getting thinner? Don't I wish. Max's eyes bounced off mine. Lydia said, "We think one of the Cyborgs stole my notebook."

"Not Hugh," Prairie said. Her eyes narrowed.

"No, not Hugh," I quickly agreed. "We think it was probably Ashley, but we can't find it in her desk, so we figured she's probably passing it around."

"Right." Lydia pushed her glasses up her nose.

"It's not here," Max mumbled as she shoved Hugh's books back inside his desk. "Let's try Rooney's."

"Now, wait a minute," I said.

Everyone looked at me. "He doesn't have it," I said.

"How do you know?" Lydia asked.

My cheeks flared. "I just know. Even if it was offered to him, he wouldn't take it."

"S-same with Hugh," Prairie said.

"So, Jenny." Lydia smirked. "Are you in love with Kevin Rooney?"

I clucked. "Get real." To remove her bloodsucking

eyes from my face, I added, "Go ahead. Look. You won't find it."

All the time they searched Kevin's desk, Prairie and I stood back, arms folded. "It's not here," Lydia said.

"No duh," I said back. "Look, if Ashley took it, she still has it. She probably stashed it somewhere, like in her bra."

"I'm not looking there," Max said.

Prairie giggled.

"In fact," I continued, "she's probably reading it to everyone in the cafeteria at this very moment."

Lydia gasped. "You may be right, Jenny. Why don't I go buy a hot lunch and check it out. You guys keep searching around the room. It's a pink spiral. With the name of our science project in purple puffy paint on the front. You can't miss it."

As Lydia yanked open the door, Max called across to her, "Bring me back some chocolate milk."

I called, "And an extra hunk of spice cake."

They all looked at me. "For Harley," I whimpered.

Chapter 13

Lydia's mom was not what I expected. I expected someone tall, like a dancer, with rock-solid thighs. Instead, she was short, like a shrimp, with flabby thighs. I could tell because she wore shorts. The only thing tall was her hair. Teased to Tennessee. Even more surprising, she had this soft voice. And she seemed nice. Obviously Lydia had inherited her father's genes. Not that Lydia wasn't nice; she just had a terminal case of megaphone mouth.

After Dr. Marianne Beals greeted us in her sweet, soft way, Lydia hustled us back to her bedroom. "My mom said we could use any of these costumes we want, as long as we don't ruin them." Lydia lifted the lid on a large metal trunk beside her bed. Max tromped around the bed and threw herself length-wise across the frilly bedspread. No springs squeaked. "Hey," Max said. "Is this a water bed?"

"Yes," Lydia replied. "And my mom'll kill you if she sees you on it with your boots."

"Let her try," Max muttered.

"Ooh, I want this!" Prairie pulled out a pink feather boa and draped it around her neck.

"Yeah, and I'll take this." I removed a leopard-spotted bodysuit, size one. Lydia opened her mouth to say it, but I saved her the embarrassment. "Just kidding. Unless I wear it on my head." It snapped into place, and I flung the legs and arms back like long dreadlocks. Prairie and Lydia hyena-howled.

Prairie said, "Ooh, Max, this is d-definitely you." She unfolded a red silk cape with matching mask. Two little devil's horns stuck up from the top of the mask. Max's eyebrows arched.

"I have dibs on this," Lydia said. She grabbed a long, skinny rod from the bottom of the trunk. With a flick of the wrist, she unleashed it. A Japanese fan arced across her face.

"Gorgeous," Prairie breathed.

There were enough sequins in that trunk to spark a fireworks display. After we pawed through all the costumes, Lydia said, "Okay, Prairie. You're first.

Pick out an outfit. Then come sit at my vanity table and I'll do your hair and makeup."

While Lydia brushed out Prairie's braids, I loaded up on flashy jewelry. Even though none of the outfits would fit, there was enough chiffon to wrap around my bulk several times.

A knock sounded on the door. "Get that, Jenny," Lydia said. A row of bobby pins fell out of her mouth.

I hopped across the room and opened the door. Lydia's mom asked, "How's it going in here?"

"Good," I answered.

She glanced at my getup and smiled. "Can I help with makeup or anything?"

I twisted my head toward Lydia. She'd teased Prairie's hair into a giant haystack and stuck a peacock headdress on top. It looked like there'd been a barnyard brawl, and the rooster lost. "Uh, maybe—"

"No," Lydia cut me off. "We're fine." She met Prairie's panicked eyes in the mirror and added, "Well, maybe, if you're not too busy. I guess I could use a little help with the hair."

"You know I'm never too busy for you." Lydia's mom frowned at her. "Or your friends."

Lydia gave me a look like "Puh-leaze."

Dr. Beals padded in barefoot and took the brush from Lydia. We watched as she styled Prairie's hair into a big bouffant and curled her bangs with a curling iron. Obviously she'd had a lot of practice with that look. As Lydia's mom fitted the headdress in place, Prairie said in a sigh, "It m-must be fun being a Las V-Vegas showgirl."

"Not really," Lydia's mom said. "It's too much work for too little money. And the hours stink." She told us how she worked all night, then studied for college until three or four A.M. Afterward she slept for a couple of hours, then got up to practice for a new show or prepare for the next performance. "What a life." She shook her head. "I don't miss it."

Behind her, Lydia faked violin playing.

Prairie sighed again. "I'd like to t-try it."

"Me, too," I said.

"Yeah, right." Lydia rolled her eyes.

Her mother whirled and shot Lydia a dirty look. "Whatever you can do or dream you can, begin it. Boldness has genius, power, and magic in it. Goethe," she quoted.

"You go, girl. Oprah," I quoted back.

She laughed. And I didn't even have to explain the joke, like I did with Dr. Sid sometimes. A thought struck me. I wished Lydia's mom was my therapist. I bet she could solve my problem.

"There we go," she said to Prairie. "What do you

think?" With a final flourish, she brushed blusher across Prairie's cheekbones and stepped back. Prairie gazed into the mirror. She licked her pink lemonade lips and smiled. "G-gosh" was all she could say.

"Prairie, you're beautiful," Lydia said. "Hugh won't know what hit him."

That perked Max up. "Hit who?"

Lydia's mom said, "Okay, who's next?"

We scrabbled to get in line. Even Max, although what she wanted wasn't exactly your classic glamour makeover. A few minutes later, smiling through black lipstick and electrified frizz, Max spun on the vanity seat and pronounced, "Shazam."

"Scary," I mumbled.

Lydia was made up to resemble a Japanese geisha girl, in a silk kimono with her hair wound in a bun. Two glittery silver chopsticks stuck out each side of the bun.

Dr. Beals suggested I play an Arabian harem girl. With all that chiffon, it was perfect. She gelled my hair in waxy waves all over my head and outlined my lips with ruby red lipstick. Thick eyeliner and thicker mascara made me look like the Queen of Sheba, whatever she looks like.

"Let me take the pictures," Max said. "My brother taught me how to use a camera."

Prairie didn't have a problem with that. She retrieved the camera and film from her backpack and handed them to Max. While Max loaded the film, Lydia said, "We need a backdrop. A chair against the wall or something."

"I know." Lydia's mom snapped her fingers. "Follow me."

She led us to her bedroom and a comfy overstuffed armchair. At least it would've been comfy if there hadn't been a ton of trashy romance novels on top of it. Stacking the books on the floor, she said, "Lydia, go get that set of black silk sheets from the back of the linen closet." Smiling at us, she added, "I knew I'd use those sheets again someday." Her gaze strayed over our heads and down the hall. She seemed kind of sad. The way Mom did sometimes when I caught her alone.

We draped the sheets over the chair, where Prairie posed like Cleopatra. Max snapped shots from all different angles. Then Lydia lounged across the cushion, pretending to be all sexy. I took over where she left off. Lydia's mom cracked up. She said drama was my true calling. We were all giggling pretty good, but when Max posed like a demented demon, with that cape and mask, we literally screamed. Dr. Beals got such a stitch in her side, I thought we might have to call an ambulance.

Too soon the film was gone. Lydia's mom said, "I don't know about you all, but I'm famished. I bought snacks; they're out in the kitchen."

We nearly trampled each other getting there. Okay, I nearly trampled everyone. On the dining-room table was a tray of assorted pastries; cut-out cakes and cream puffs, chocolate eclairs, frosted cookies. Drool pooled at my feet. I felt sick. All the willpower in the world couldn't keep me from those cream puffs.

Lydia said, "I hope you brought your food diary, Jenny." She turned to her mom. "I forgot to tell you, Mom. Jenny's on a diet."

My face flared. "It's not a diet. It's a nutrition plan."

Dr. Beals frowned. "Why? You look perfectly fine to me."

Not only did I want her for my therapist, I wanted her for my mother.

Chapter 14

"**D**ad, could I go to another child psychologist?" I asked him on Sunday afternoon while I helped stuff dirty clothes into the washer downstairs.

He poured about a gallon of liquid Cheer into the tub and closed the lid. "Why? You don't like Dr. Sid?"

"I don't think Dr. Sid is really helping me with my . . . problem. I mean, I haven't lost any weight. In fact, I gained three pounds over the weekend." He didn't need to know about the pastry orgy at Lydia's.

"I believe the idea is for you to help yourself." Over the empty laundry basket, Dad met my eyes.

"It is?" I threw up my hands. "See? Why didn't he say that? Instead he has me seeing this anorexic dietician and keeping this stupid food diary. Which I would be embarrassed to show anyone." Which I lied about losing and hadn't written in for days. "It's dumb."

Dad sighed. He brushed by me and started up the stairs. "So, what do you want to do?"

"See another psychologist. Like I said. There's this lady I know, Dr. Beals. I'd really like to go to her." There was danger in this request, I knew. The possibility existed that everyone would find out I was seeing a shrink. Not the Snob Squad so much; they'd understand. I'm talking about everyone in school. Ashley, Melanie, Mrs. Jonas, Kevin. Kevin? "Uh, never mind," I said.

"No, wait." Dad twisted around at the top of the stairs. He sighed. "I'm not totally convinced these so-called professionals are worth what they charge. But hey, if you think someone else could help you, let's do it."

"I don't know." My eyes strayed out the back door. Two mourning doves cuddled together in the crab apple tree, cooing. "Maybe it isn't the therapist. Maybe it's me, like you said." I dodged under the laundry basket and waddled away. "Guess I'm just defective."

"Don't say that."

I headed for my room.

"Jenny?" Dad called after me. "Let's talk about this."

I shut the door, and shut him out. In my room I stuck on my earphones and rusted out my brain to heavy metal music.

On Monday morning, Prairie brought the pictures to school. "Overnight p-processing," she said. "They cost six dollars and forty-nine cents. Plus the film, it c-comes to about two dollars and fifty cents each."

Lydia and I scrounged in our purses and paid up. Max said, "I owe you."

"No p-problem. You gotta see these. C-come on."

We jammed into the girls' restroom and shut the door. "Open it. Hurry," Lydia said. She was so excited, I thought she'd wet her pants. We were in the right place, anyway.

Slowly, carefully, Prairie lifted the flap of the photo envelope. She reached inside and pulled out the first picture.

"Oh, my God!" Lydia shrieked over Prairie's shoulder. She wrenched the picture out of Prairie's hand. "My God. If anyone sees this, I'll be the laughingstock of school."

You already are, I almost said. Maybe I did. "Let me see."

"No way." Lydia slapped the picture against her chest.

"It can't be that bad."

"There's m-m-ore," Prairie sang. She showed us another one of Lydia, and we howled.

Lydia grabbed the picture and cringed. "All right." She took a deep breath and narrowed her eyes. "Let's see the rest of you."

Prairie passed around the stack of photos. My glamour photos were, in a word, hideous. Worse than hideous. I looked like a hussy, humpback hippopotamus. In ballet pink, if you can imagine.

When Max saw her first picture, she smirked. "Bad," she said. "Really bad."

She loved them. Hers were the only ones that did anyone justice.

After we got over the initial shock, we all agreed that a couple of Prairie's glamour photos weren't horrible. In fact, they were pretty good. The ones in focus anyway. She looked radiant. Sparkling, at least, with all the sequins. We took a few minutes to vote on our favorite, the one we'd sneak to Hugh.

A rush of air blew through the bathroom door as someone opened it. Max charged over to wedge it shut with a shoulder. "Hey, I need to go," some girl yelled.

"Go away," Max growled. "It's a private party."

"We can put the picture in Hugh's lunch box," Lydia said. "He always brings his lunch."

In an insulated, zip-up lunch box with matching Thermos. You get the picture.

"N-no." Prairie's eyes filled with terror. "We c-can't do it at school. I d-don't want anyone to see my picture. I mean, anyone besides Hugh."

Lydia tapped an index finger on her lips. "Maybe we could find out where he lives and send the picture to him."

Prairie said, "I know where he lives."

We all stared at her. Her face flared. In a tiny voice she said, "Hugh's my next-door neighbor."

Okay, granted, the Solanos were not bosom buddies with their next-door neighbors. The Crotchety Crockerds on the south scolded me once in public when I accidentally left my Barbie bride doll in their driveway. Old man Crotchety crushed it flat with his classic Chrysler. Then he had the gall to holler at me when I started screaming, "Murderer! Murderer!" We hadn't spoken to them for six years.

To the north side loomed a hash house. At least that's what Dad called it. More people came and went at midnight than the drive-up window at

Wendy's. So I can understand how Prairie and Hugh had never once talked, even though he'd moved in next door to her the summer before fifth grade.

Still, it was weird. She said Hugh and her brother Sun were friends, and that Hugh came over after dinner sometimes to surf the Internet with Sun. Imagine having your one true love in the same house. Close enough to smell his sweat. Which Hugh had plenty of.

We decided to stick Prairie's picture in an envelope and address it to Hugh. Anonymous like. Then, after school, Prairie'd slip the envelope in the Torkersons' mailbox.

We offered to help Prairie deliver the photo, but she said no thanks. I think she wanted us as far away from Hugh's house as possible. Which was fine with me. If we got caught, she'd hate us forever. Prairie wasn't worried, though. She said as soon as Hugh came over to surf the Net, she could sneak out and do it. I wondered if she really would.

Lydia said, "Do you mind if I take the other pictures home tonight? My mom wanted to see how they turned out."

The bell rang, and we scrambled. Hastily Prairie stuck the stack of photos back into the envelope and handed it to Lydia. I should've protested. As leader of the Snob Squad, it's my duty to protect our reputations. Maybe not our current reputations, but any future ones we might acquire. I should've offered to stash the pictures until school was out. Or have Max stash them. Nobody'd mess with her. But I didn't. I just let Lydia drop them in her book bag. Bad move.

Chapter 15

The catastrophe occurred during language arts. First hour. As we got up to fetch our books from the book rack, Lydia, renowned klutz of the cosmos, tripped over her chair, bounced off my body, and butt-crashed into Melanie Mason's desk. Which tipped over backward, taking out the desk behind it and knocking Lydia's book bag to the floor. Where the photo envelope flew out and skidded across the rug. Guess where? Straight onto Ashley Krupps's fat feet. As if in slow-motion replay, I watched Ashley pick up the package, open it, and drop her jaw to shriek.

Naturally everyone had to see what the ruckus was about. Lydia threw a hyper hissy fit, but not before the photos had made it around the room—over our outstretched hands and behind our backs. Everyone whooped.

I've never been so embarrassed. I take that back. The time my lunch sack ripped and a hundred malted milk balls bounced out was pretty humiliating. Especially since most of them rolled to a stop under Kevin Rooney's Reeboks.

Eventually Mrs. Jonas intervened. Even though she stifled a guffaw when she caught a glimpse of the pictures, she got them back to us. So much for the glory of glamour photos. By recess we were all the laughingstock of Montrose Middle School. So what else is new?

"Harley looks sick," I said during science. We'd just finished putting him through his paces. At least Max was trying to finish. Every couple of seconds Harley would stop and lean, like the Tower of Pizza. Where is the Tower of Pizza? I'd like to live there. Anyway, Harley looked like he was ready to faint. Can a rat faint? As if in answer to my question, Harley shivered all over and flopped flat.

"He's just beat," Max said. "Give him a break."

"Maybe we should splash cold water on his face," Lydia suggested.

We all stared at her. The stares turned to glares.

"Look, I said I was sorry about the pictures, okay?" Her eyes welled with tears.

My eyes dropped. Next to me, Prairie took a deep breath. Her hand reached up to grasp Lydia's limp shoulder, and she said, "It's n-not your fault. Any one of us c-could've done it."

"Yeah, but we didn't," muttered Max.

I shot her a warning look. She folded her arms.

"At least you weren't posing like some airhead on *Baywatch*," Lydia snapped.

"True," Max said, which only made Lydia feel worse.

"W well," Prairie piped up. "At least I don't have to leave my picture in Hugh's mailbox now." She sighed. The memory of what had happened in class resurfaced, and we all shuddered. After Melanie handed the pictures to Kevin, he smiled and passed them on. To Hugh. Hugh's eyes grew big as black holes before he fixed them on Prairie. If I'd had a shovel, I would've dug her a hole to crawl in. Right behind me.

"Hey, it's over, okay?" I said. "We're ruined. Big deal. We have a lot of experience at this. As long as no one sells our glamour photos to the *National Enquirer*, I think we still have a future in high school."

Max snorted.

"Thank you, Jenny," Lydia said. "So, does anyone have a notebook I can borrow the rest of the week until the science fair on Saturday? I better document the fact that Harley's sick."

"He's not sick," Max said. "There, look, he reached the end."

It was true. On his own, Harley had followed my trail of stale spice cake crumbs to the end of the course. Suddenly he leaned, rocked unsteadily, and rolled right into the siren's green button.

The blare registered about a bejillion decibels in the confined science lab. Anyone within earshot was instantly hearing impaired. A bunch of girls screamed. Everyone else covered their ears. I hollered, "Tornado! Take cover!"

Just as we'd practiced since kindergarten, everyone hit the deck and rolled under the tables, covering their heads. Except us. We just stood there and hyena-howled at the goons. Revenge is so sweet.

Later that afternoon, I confronted Ashley about Lydia's notebook. For some reason I felt it was my responsibility to get it back. Maybe I was afraid Lydia would try and there'd be a brawl in the bathroom. "Hey, Ashley," I said casually as we passed going to and from the pencil sharpener. "I believe you have something that belongs to us. "

She blew off her shavings. "Such as?"

"I think you know."

I thought I could do the blank, though obviously guilty, look better than anyone, but Ashley's was good.

"If you don't give it back, I'm telling Mr. Biekmund." She just looked at me. Then her eyes crossed, and she imitated a moron. Very realistic. She sniffed the air and said, "I think I smell a rat. A big, fat one. And I don't mean the one in the cage." She puckered her nose and waddled away.

I almost stabbed her in the butt with my pencil. I should have. How much lead does it take for lead poisoning?

As soon as Mom and Dad left for their marriage counseling, Vanessa and I ordered a pizza. Mom's curried corn quesadillas didn't exactly stick to the ribs. Ever wonder where the expression "food to die for" came from? Now you know.

While we channel surfed, we stuffed our faces. Okay, I stuffed mine. But it was the first time in a long time that Vanessa actually ate more than three bites.

We settled on Nick at Nite, which was having a mini-marathon of back-to-back *Brady Bunch* reruns.

Out of nowhere, Vanessa said, "I bet Mom and Dad are going to get a divorce."

I froze, a pizza slice poised midair on its way to my open mouth. "What do you mean?" I managed to croak.

She turned to me. "I mean d-i-v-o-r-s-e."

She couldn't spell any better than me. "They can't," I said. "They're in marriage counseling. It's against the law or something to get divorced while you're getting help."

"What help?" Vanessa said. "They argue all the time, in case you haven't noticed. They hate each other."

"They do not!" The mozzarella in my stomach melded into a hard cheese ball. "They hate us."

Van met my eyes. She blinked back to *The Brady Bunch*, who were having a pleasant family discussion during dinner. Alice, the maid, carted in a luscious-looking chocolate cake. Maybe that's what we needed. A maid.

"They'll work it out," I said. "They always do."

"I don't think so," Vanessa countered. "Ever since Mom went to work and Dad lost his job, things have changed."

That's it! That's when everything changed. But

why? I answered my own question: "Because they've lost the romance. But they can find it again."

"What?" Vanessa curled a lip at me.

My face flared. I must've said that out loud. "Nothing." Quickly I added, "Everyone changes. You've changed. I've changed. Change is good. Through change people grow."

She widened her eyes at me like I was a raging retard. "Who taught you the facts of life?"

"You did."

"I got it wrong." She turned back to the Bradys. A commercial came on, and she said, "I hate to tell you this, Jenny. You're living in a dreamworld. Wake up. I want you to be prepared for the worst."

Why does everyone always say that? Why can't we be prepared for the best?

Just then the garage door sounded. A few seconds later, car doors slammed and the back door opened. Dad's voice echoed through the kitchen, "I'm just saying I think it's a waste of money. We're paying a bloody fortune for this guy to sit and stare at us for an hour every week."

"You're not paying a penny," Mom snarled. "The cost of all this counseling is coming out of my insurance. Since I'm the only one working."

The sofa creaked. I glanced over to see that Vanessa had curled into the corner of the couch, hugging her knees. Her eyes were transfixed on the TV. I'd had about as much of *The Brady Bunch* as I could stomach. Speaking of stomachs . . . I tossed my half-eaten slice of pizza back into the box, closed the cover, and escaped with it to my room for a brain-numbing blast of heavy metal music and mozzarella.

Chapter 16

The next morning as Lydia, Max, Prairie, and I were heading for class, someone shouted, "Hey, guys. Wait." That someone was Hugh. We all stopped and turned. Hugh smacked right into my back, almost as if he meant to. Weirdo. Something sharp, his slide rule probably, stuck in my spine. Go ahead, I thought, add physical pain to my emotional and psychological distress.

"Sorry," Hugh mumbled.

"Want to get off my foot?" I said.

He stepped back. "I, uh . . ." He gulped. "Do you mind if I talk to . . . to Prairie?"

"No," Lydia said. "Go ahead."

Bunching up Lydia's polyester sleeve in one hand

and Max's canvas camouflage jacket in the other, I said, "He means alone."

"Oh," Lydia replied.

I yanked Lydia and Max ahead. Prairie smiled gratefully at me.

We couldn't hear them, but we did see Hugh write something down and nod before he plodded off. Prairie just stood there, gaping. We bustled back to her.

"Well?" Lydia attacked her. "What did he want? Did he ask you to the dance?"

"N-no."

"Well, did he mention the glamour photos?"

"Y-yes." Prairie's eyes filled with tears.

Lydia squeezed her arm. "Did he say something about them? Something mean?"

"N-no." She sniffled. "He thought they were b-beautiful."

"He must need an emergency eye exam," I mumbled.

Lydia said, "What else did he want? What did he write down?"

Prairie bit her bottom lip. "He wanted J-Jenny's phone number."

They all looked at me.

"Huh? Why would he want my number?"

Lydia's eyes narrowed. "Why else?" she snarled. "He's going to ask *you* to the dance!"

I heard Prairie tell Mrs. Jonas she wanted to skip science and spend the whole day in the resource room, catching up on assignments. Quickly I rushed over to the pencil sharpener so that I could talk to her before she left. So that I could tell her I wasn't interested in Hugh Torkerson. Get real. But when Prairie saw me waiting there, she deliberately went out the long way, through the back door.

Sometimes life stinks. Like most of the time, if you believed Vanessa. Which I was beginning to. Prairie hated me. And I didn't blame her. I blamed Lydia. "This is all your fault," I told her on the way to the science lab. "You just had to play Cupid. Stupid, stupid Cupid."

"I didn't do anything," Lydia flared. "You're the one who was flirting with Hugh."

I shoved her against the lockers. "I was not!"

Max stepped between us. "Cool it," she said. "You're gonna get us busted."

Lydia stretched her neck out around Max's arm. "This was all your idea, Jenny."

"My idea!"

"You're the one who thought up Herd a Nerd."

"Well, *you* had to take glamour photos."

Lydia clucked. "That was Max's idea."

We both glared up at Max.

"Shut up," she growled. "It's all our faults. We shoulda just butted out."

I took a deep breath. "Max is right. We never should've gotten involved in Prairie's love life. All for one, and one for all. What a crock."

Lydia hung her head.

"Look, it's my fault, okay?" I said. I was their leader. I was responsible.

Lydia must've taken it the wrong way. "So you *are* interested in Hugh. You admit it."

"I do not!" I cried. "And I'm not flirting with him, either. God. Tork the Dork?"

"He's not that bad," Lydia said. "In fact, the more I get to know him, the more I think he's not all that dorky."

"Maybe *you're* interested," Max said.

Lydia sneered at her. "I'm not, believe me. But I think Ashley is. For real."

We all considered that scenario. Scary scene.

"Question is," Lydia said, "is he interested in her?"

That might be Lydia's question. Mine was, Why is he asking for my phone number?

What Prairie missed during science class was Harley hip-hopping through the obstacle course perfectly, from start to finish, without a fleck of food for reinforcement. Three times in a row he set off the siren. After the second run, the whole class watched and cheered Harley on. Except Ashley and Melanie, of course. They scowled at us from the PC center. Hugh and Kevin joined everyone else in fawning over Harley. A couple of times I thought I caught Hugh trying to inch closer to me, but I kept a wide berth. They don't call me Wide Bertha for nothing.

The Beak Man said our project was excellent. That it actually gave our school a chance at a prize. Then he asked if we couldn't disconnect the siren because it was giving him a major migraine.

After school we joined forces to look for Prairie. To talk to her, to try to convince her that I wasn't a threat. That Hugh couldn't possibly be interested in me. And if he was, he was blinder than I thought.

When we turned down the A-wing hallway, we spotted Prairie outside the resource room. She was just standing there, staring up at the wall. "Hey,

Prairie," I called. "We missed you at science. You should've seen Harley, the wonder rat. He ran the obstacle course three times." Maybe if I pretended everything was normal, it would be. Denial, I know. It didn't work with my parents; I don't know why I thought it would with my friends.

Prairie didn't reply. Didn't even turn our way. Great. She hated me.

As we got closer, Max said, "Whatcha doin', Prayer?"

She sighed, a heavy sigh, full of resignation. We gathered around her. Our eyes followed hers to the wall.

My stomach lurched.

The poster read,

Sixth-Grade Spring Fling
Friday, May 15
We're puttin' on the Ritz (so bring a box of crackers).
Just kidding.
Shirt and shoes required.

"Oh, brother." Lydia rolled her eyes. "Who thought up that stupid slogan?"

No one answered.

Prairie sighed again. So did I. She met my eyes.

Just as I opened my mouth to speak, Lydia said, "Oh, figures." She pointed down the hall. There were Ashley and Melanie, taping a poster to the A-wing window. After they finished, they had to walk by us to get out.

Ashley stopped to sneer. "Not that you'd care," she said, "but we're having a live band come and play at the dance. The Eight Anchovies."

Where had I heard that? Lydia's fiery eyes met mine. Now I remembered. The survey. Before Lydia could splutter a curse, Ashley added, "Me and Mel asked Hugh and Kev to the dance. Since we're teammates and all. Oh, by the way, no fourth graders allowed."

Lydia's hair frizzed from the roots to the split ends.

Ashley smirked. She knew she'd gotten Lydia.

Lydia blurted, "I heard Hugh's asking Jenny. He's calling her tonight."

I almost peed my pants.

Ashley said, "Where'd you hear that?"

Lydia shrugged. "Around."

"She's lying," I said. "Don't believe it." I'd strangle Lydia. Right after Max beat her to a pulp, if the growling next to me meant what I thought it meant.

Ashley and Prairie had the same expression on their faces. Like they were about to burst into tears.

And I was the bimbo who broke their hearts over Hugh. Melanie grabbed Ashley's arm and said, "C'mon, Ash. Let's go hang the rest of these posters."

I glanced at Prairie. She looked as pale as I felt. Then I glared at Lydia.

She began, "I just thought—"

"He's not asking me, Prairie," I cut her off. "It's a joke or something."

Prairie shook her head. "Hugh n-never jokes." She whirled and walked away.

Max ripped the poster off the wall and crushed it to dust under her army boot.

"Me next," I said.

Chapter 17

Mom made something called Singapore stir-fry for dinner. You've never eaten foreign food until you've had Singapore stir-fry. I kept staring at my mound of rice, expecting something to squirm.

Out of the silence, Dad cleared his throat. "Hear ye, hear ye," he said.

"We hear ye," I muttered.

"The first official Solano self-therapy session is now in order."

We all stared at him. I said, "Is this *The People's Court?*"

That elicited an almost detectable wave of amusement. Dad replied, "In a way. Except we are the judge and jury. From now on, no more shrinks. We're going to solve our own problems. Here, during dinner. It's my belief that all of our problems can be summed up in one word: *communication*. Or lack of it. So, would anyone like to share?"

Vanessa and I looked at each other. In unison we shoved our plates of Singapore stir-fry at him.

He clucked, and shoved them back. "Get serious."

"We are serious," we said together, and giggled. Maybe this was going to work. Except that beside me, Mom bristled.

Whoops.

Dad said, "Come on, guys. Let's get everything out on the table."

I snapped my fingers. "I *thought* something was missing. Dessert. Where is it? In the freezer?"

Vanessa smothered her smirk with a hand.

Mother was not amused. She set her fork down hard and said, "Your father's right about one thing, Jenny. Apparently your counseling is a waste of time and money. You don't seem to be losing any weight. Whatever happened to the food diary you were supposed to be keeping?"

"I have it," I mumbled.

"Well, let's see it."

I gasped. "It's private." It's empty, I almost said.

Mom exhaled wearily. "I've tried to help, you

know. I've stuck to the dietician's meal plan reli-giously. But all you do is turn up your nose at every meal."

"No, it's my stomach that turns," I said.

"Jenny!" Dad barked.

"Well, it's true. This food is totally inedible."

Mom's jaw came unhinged.

"Well, I'm sorry, but it is. If you don't believe me, ask Vanessa." I turned to her. She turned to stone. Didn't even come to my rescue. Thanks a lot, I seethed to myself. To Mom I said, "How come you're always ragging on me about my eating problems? What about Vanessa's? She's anorexic, in case you haven't noticed."

Through sunken eye sockets, Vanessa glared at me. "Why should I eat?" she said. "You eat enough for the both of us."

"Vanessa!" Mom scolded.

Vanessa blinked at me and looked away.

Mom said, "We know Vanessa has a problem. We're working on it . . . in private."

"Oh, great," I said. "And my problem we get to work on in public."

Mom dropped her gaze.

It got real quiet. Finally Vanessa shattered the silence. "Jenny's right," she said. "Everyone in this family has an eating disorder. You know why? Because this food is terrible."

"Vanessa!" Dad barked.

I sent Van a mental message: Thank you.

Mom's eyes darted around the table. They held on Dad. He opened his mouth, then shut it. Mom's eyes welled with tears. "It's not easy, you know, having to work all day, then come home and cook and clean house—"

"You don't clean house," Dad said. "I do."

Mom sniffled. "Well, I would if you didn't do it." She blew her nose in a napkin. Her voice trembling, she whimpered, "I try to be a good mother."

"You are," Vanessa and I said together.

Dad frowned at Mom. "Who said you weren't a good mother?"

Mom shook her head.

Dad continued, "None of us has ever felt you weren't a good mother. Or a good wife. Or a good anything. We appreciate everything you do. Don't we, girls?" Dad widened his eyes at us.

"We do," we both chorused.

"I'm the one who's not appreciated." Dad folded his arms.

We all gaped at him.

He unfolded his arms and started waving them

around. "I do all the housework, the laundry, the shopping. I pay the bills. I'd cook if you'd let me. I know you don't think it's enough, that I should work full-time, too."

Mom countered, "I never said that. I think you do plenty. It's a lot of work, keeping this house running. I should know—I did it for the first ten years of our marriage. The laundry alone is a full-time job."

"It sure is," Dad muttered.

"I do appreciate it," Mom said meekly.

"Me, too," Vanessa and I put in.

Mom added, "I wish I could do more."

"Why?" Dad rested his hands on the table. "I thought you hated housework."

"I do," Mom said. "But I still feel guilty."

"About what? Working? You love your job. You didn't go to college at night for six years so you could iron my shirts." He reached over and covered her hand with his. "You don't have to feel guilty, hon," he spoke softly. "To tell you the truth, I kind of enjoy housework. More than I ever did office work. In fact, I'm getting a T-shirt that says, *Laundry is my life*." He smiled.

Through taut lips, Mom cracked a smile.

Dad sobered fast. "If anyone should feel guilty, it's me," he said. "Having you support the family, work all the time, come home exhausted, cook dinner, it's . . . it's hard for me."

Vanessa looked at me. She must've been thinking the same thing I was; that this was the longest conversation our parents had ever had.

Mom's hand turned over and squeezed Dad's. "I know it's hard," she said through a sniffle. "And I don't really care if you never go back to work, Robert. It's a relief knowing you're home, taking care of things."

"Really?" Dad looked shocked. He cocked his head and said, "Wow, I guess we should talk about this."

Mom nodded. "I guess we should."

He put his arm around her shoulders. "I want you to laugh more. Especially at my jokes."

Mom laughed.

That's it. I stood up. "If you're going to get all mushy, can I be excused? I have a delicate stomach, you know."

Vanessa rose. "I have no stomach."

Mom and Dad sucked in smiles.

Vanessa followed me down the hall, muttering, "Especially for Singapore stir-fry."

"See?" I said, pausing at her bedroom door. "They'll work it out. Mr. Mom and Mrs. Dad. How romantic."

Vanessa made a face at me. "How weird, you mean."

A thought barreled through my brain. "You think we could get on *Oprah*? Yesterday she had a show called 'Families Who Wave Their Dirty Underwear in Public.' Ours could be 'Families Who Don't Have Dirty Underwear.' We could show Dad doing the laundry."

Vanessa didn't reply. She was gazing into space, looking spaced out, as usual.

"Earth to Van." I snapped my fingers in front of her face.

She caught my hand. "I have a plan," she said.

My stomach lurched. Why did the word *plan* suddenly make me want to scream?

Vanessa glanced back toward the kitchen, where Mom and Dad were huddled, whispering together. Vanessa pointed to my bedroom door. "You got anything edible in there?" she said.

"Just a moldy package of Hostess cupcakes."

"Perfect." She shoved me inside and shut the door behind us.

Chapter 18

On Saturday morning, I woke up with a fluttery stomach. It wasn't Vanessa's plan that was making me anxious. Well, maybe a little. If it backfired, we might both be put up for adoption. But we weren't putting the plan into action until Sunday night. No, this anxiety was imminent. I think I was excited about the science fair.

How dumb.

When the horn honked outside, I'd already been ready for half an hour. Max had bribed Scuzz-Gut into hauling the Extreme Rat-o-rama to Hinckley High School and picking me up on the way. Knowing how Scuzz-Gut drove, I buckled up tighter than a twist tie and said a silent prayer. Talk about queasy.

Half an hour of road rage later, Scuzz-Gut squealed

into a handicapped parking place right up front. I didn't figure it was my duty to mention the absence of a handicapped parking sticker. Whoever was stupid enough to stop him was risking a rumble.

It took about an hour to find our class in the mob scene inside. Dozens of areas were designated for the fair. Hundreds maybe. After the bejillionth time Scuzz-Gut growled, "I ain't haulin' this rat contraption another inch," we heard Lydia holler. She has this real loud voice; you can't miss it. Beside her, Prairie flagged us down. I was glad to see that Prairie had come. Even though she was still one of us, lately it didn't feel like she was one *with* us. Know what I mean?

At our designated spot, Scuzz-Gut dropped off the Rat-o-rama, literally, and said to Max, "You got the rat?"

She showed him Harley's carrier.

"Okay," he said. "Break a leg." He punched Max in the arm and blew out of there. What a sweet guy. While Max and Prairie set up, I said to Lydia, "Come on, let's find the food."

On the way out, I asked, "Where's your mom? I thought you said she was coming."

Lydia smiled. "She had to work today, so she dropped me off. Thank gawd."

Maybe being a psychologist's daughter was as bad as being the principal's daughter. Maybe worse, since the person looking over your shoulder was a trained professional.

Lydia yawned. "I was up till midnight working on our project."

I frowned. "What do you mean?"

"I had to redo the whole notebook," she said. "Since I never did find it. Since we know who's got it."

"Yeah. Ashley was probably trying to sabotage our project. Not that we'd ever do that to *her*."

Lydia smirked. "We don't have to."

I wondered what she meant but didn't get a chance to ask, because we were swallowed up by the swarm of people following the signs to the Hinckley High Future Homemakers of America's concession stand. When we got there, Lydia answered my question before I could ask. "Did you see the Cyber Stars' project?"

I shook my head.

"Well, as of yesterday they still couldn't get the two computers talking. And it's such a ridiculous idea, naming one Barbie and the other Ken. They're supposed to have a conversation. First Barbie says, 'Hello, Ken. How are you?' Then Ken says something like, 'Fine. You're lookin' bad, babe. Real bad.' Then Barbie goes, 'Oh, wow, Ken. You're hot, too.' "

I looked at Lydia like she had a memory malfunction. "Serious?" I said.

"Serious. At least that's what's supposed to happen, except Barbie doesn't get a word out before she freezes up. Then the whole system crashes." Lydia laughed.

That scenario was realistic, at least. If I was Barbie and Kevin was Ken, I'd freeze up, too.

Lydia wheezed, "Don't you think it's funny?"

"Yeah," I said. "A real scream. Do you want chocolate or coconut?" I surveyed the doughnut choices. Six doughnuts for a dollar. Not bad, even if most of them resembled deformed dumplings. Whoever married these future homemakers of America were in for a dining disaster.

"We'd like three chocolate and three coconut," I ordered without waiting for Lydia to make up her mind. The zitty FHAer and I exchanged a greasy bag and a buck.

"I hope Harley likes coconut," Lydia said. "You're not supposed to give animals chocolate, you know."

My mind reeled. Had I fed Harley anything chocolate? I couldn't remember. I started to chomp into a chocolate doughnut. Suddenly my anxiety resurged and I lost my appetite. Handing the doughnut to Lydia, I said, "Speaking of Harley, did you see how he was leaning yesterday? Worse than the day before."

Lydia licked off a drip of chocolate. "Max says he's fine, but I don't know. Harley looks sick. He's wheezing a lot, like I do when I get an asthma attack."

"Maybe he's allergic to science, too. Maybe we should ask the Beak Man if we could borrow his snot rag."

"Jenny!" Lydia whapped me and laughed.

I was glad we were friends. Lydia could be so much fun. As we meandered back to the gym, taking in the sights, sounds, and smells, I thought, Science fairs are fascinating. Besides the food, there was more nerdiness concentrated in one locale than at a computer convention. I felt out of place. Not to mention out of my intellectual element. "Lydia, could I borrow your glasses?" I asked her. "I feel underdressed."

"Huh?" she said, scanning her pink paisley outfit.

"Never mind."

The judging had already started by the time we got back. "You're next," Mr. Biekmund said to us. "After the Cyber Stars." He seemed nervous as a ninny. "Are you ready to go? Where's Harley?"

"He's resting," Max said.

"Ps-psyching himself up," Prairie added.

The Beak Man smiled a sick smile. "Good luck," he said in a sniffle. "Have I told you how proud I am of you all?"

We all looked vacant.

"No, really," he said. "You'll each get an A in science this term. The Extreme Rat-o-rama is a super project."

"Super," I said as I eyeballed the squad. An A in science? That ought to shock my family. Shock therapy. Maybe that's what we needed.

At the table next to ours, the three judges huddled around the Cyber Stars' project. We wandered over to observe.

Hugh was explaining. "The male computer, Ken"—he blushed—"has a choice of responses to, uh, Barbie's," he mumbled, "questions. It's like artificial intelligence."

Ashley interrupted, "Except it's not artificial. It's real. They're having a real conversation. First Ken asks Barbie to the big dance and she says yes. Or vice versa." She beamed at Hugh.

He looked green. I think he was wishing she was artificial. I was, and that her batteries would die. One of the judges said, "Okay, let's see how it works."

Kevin switched on Ken. Melanie booted Barbie. Kevin keyed in, "H-e-l-l-o."

Barbie said, on the screen, "Hey, you're cute."

Ken replied, "What's your name?"

Wow, I was impressed. So were the judges, if their wide eyes were any indication.

Barbie said, "Will you call me tonight?"

Ken said, "What should I wear? Underwear?"

Huh? My eyes bugged out.

Ken added, "Are you my mother? Where is your hair?"

Barbie said, "I can't find my brain. Who's knocking on your head?"

Then they both started garbling garbage in unison. None of the sentences made sense. And they were talking so fast, it was giving me whiplash.

Barbie said, "Would you like to go to the bathroom with me?" and Ken replied, "I feel like barfing." Then he did. For real. The computer made this totally life-like barfing noise out the back, right before it crashed and burned. Barbie beeped, blooped, and blinked. Her screen went black.

The crowd fought hard to control themselves. We didn't. We hyena-howled hysterically.

If we weren't already dying of laughter, Ashley

and Melanie would've machine-gunned us down with their eyes.

"Thank you," one of the judges finally managed to squeak from a suppressed giggle. "Very, uh, innovative." The judges all marked their scorecards, or whatever they were using to grade us.

Ashley seethed, "Who put that sound in? Did you program that, Kevin? It sounds like you. I'll kill you. I swear."

I thought I saw Kevin smirk. Now you know why I think he's a god.

We were next.

Chapter 19

The four judges circled our table. Everyone else in the room jockeyed for position. Immediately Lydia started to explain our project. "I might've missed a few details because somebody stole my notebook." She glared at Ashley.

"Just show us what you have," one of the judges said.

Max retrieved Harley from his cage. Prairie and I looked at each other and gulped a big one. I could tell Prairie was nervous; her hand shook as she set the siren. Battery acid was burning up my stomach lining. "Does anyone have a Tums?" I said.

Everyone felt in their pockets. No Tums.

"Jenny, you don't look well," the Beak Man said.

"If you have to . . . you know. The restroom's . . ." He pointed.

"I'm okay," I lied. "But thanks."

As Max placed Harley in the Extreme Rat-o-rama, a group gathered. Lydia finished her explanation about rat psychology, positive reinforcement versus negative, something about tough love and therapeutic touch. Who knew what she was babbling about? "He's trained to begin on voice command," she ended. "So, whenever you're ready." Her eyes met the judges'.

The head judge yawned. "We're ready."

"One, two, three . . ."

All together we shouted, "Go!"

Everyone sucked in their breath. Harley just stood there. Or rather, he leaned there. Human heads tilted to the left, to mimic his.

"What's wrong with him?" Hugh asked behind me.

"Nothing," I snarled.

Max said, "Come on, Har. Get up, boy. This is it. The big one." She lifted him up and plopped him down.

We tried again. "Go!" we barked.

He leaned and flopped.

"Maybe he's nervous. Maybe he needs a practice run," Lydia said.

"Maybe he needs his head examined," Ashley muttered behind her. "Like his trainers."

Ooh, I wanted so bad to accidentally on purpose stomp her foot and break a toe. Think anyone would notice? The screaming might draw attention. I reached in the greasy bag and pulled out a coconut doughnut. I crumbled a hunk of it in front of the first milk carton. Harley's whiskers twitched. He rose to his feet. He snarfed up the doughnut and scrabbled ahead.

"He's off," Max announced.

Everyone bent forward to watch as Harley squeezed through the milk jug, into the oatmeal carton, and around the steering wheel. He manuevered through a Saltines box, over a halogen headlight, up a tower of toilet paper holders, and down the other side. He stopped and leaned. Then he picked up an old trail of crumbs at a tire rim and circled inside. He wiggled through a rusty coil and weaved around a maze of plastic pudding cups. At the CD speaker, the last hurdle, right before the siren, Harley stopped. He leaned left once, twice, three times. His whiskers twitched. Max whispered, "One more, baby."

Harley looked up at her. He looked at the siren.

Then he wobbled unsteadily on his legs and keeled over.

Everyone gasped. No one moved.

Max said, "Harley?" She reached down and touched his tummy. "Har?"

Nothing. Wait, something. Babies, I thought. What a time to give birth.

Harley didn't have babies. He shuddered all over, closed his eyes, and died.

Chapter 20

Poor Harley. Poor me. His death just brought everything to a head. A fat head. Mine. Because I had no doubt in my mind that I had killed Harley. He wasn't a she. And he never was pregnant. Harley died of obesity. He ate like a pig. He didn't know when to stop. Sound like someone you know?

At home I threw myself on the bed and prayed death would come quick. Harley's death was horrid enough, but what happened afterward was hideous. I had a nervous breakdown. Right there in front of a hundred thousand people, I burst into tears. Right there in front of Kevin Rooney. And the flood wouldn't stop flowing. Not through the wheezing or hiccuping or nonstop runny nose. The Beak Man had the gall to offer me his hankie. Choke me with a licorice rope.

Needless to say, we didn't win any science prize. We did bring notoriety to Montrose Middle School, however. From now on we'd be known as Home of the Dead Rats.

Through my soggy pillow, I heard a knock on my bedroom door. Dad said, "Jenny, you have a call."

"I'm busy," I blubbered.

"You okay?"

"Yeah, swell." I curled up like a caterpillar.

Dad's footsteps creaked down the hall. A few minutes later, they creaked back and I heard a note slip under my door.

With what little life I had left in me, I hauled my you-know-what up to retrieve the note. It said, *Lydia called. She asked you to meet with everyone tomorrow at noon for a farewell to Harley. You'd know where.* Dad added underneath, *Who's Harley? And where's he going?*

"Wouldn't you like to know?" I fumed. Don't ask me why I was mad at Dad. It wasn't his fault Harley was dead—or that I was fat.

Well, maybe it was. Maybe they were his defective genes making me the baby blimp of the family.

The knock sounded again. "Geez!" I muttered into my mangled sheets. Can't anyone sulk in silence around here?

It was Mom this time. "Jenny, you have a phone call."

Cripes. "Tell Lydia I'm asleep," I called. Better yet. "Tell her I'm a slug." Lydia could be such a pest.

"You may want to take this call. It sounds . . . important."

"I can't come to the phone right now, Mom," I told her. "I'm, I'm writing in my food diary, okay?"

"Writing what?" she asked. "You skipped dinner. Are you hoarding food in your room again?"

"Yes," I said. Go away, I prayed.

She sighed heavily. Finally her footsteps faded.

Poor Mom. She didn't understand. How could she? She wasn't a trained professional. She wasn't even a registered dietician. She was just a mom. Or a dad. Whichever role she played, I bet she wished she'd gotten a better cast of kids. I mean, look at us. Both losers. Especially the fat one.

Right, Jenny. Blame everyone but yourself.

"Who was that?" I said aloud, sitting up.

Eyes met eyes in the mirror. "Oh, it's you again."

Yeah, it's me again. How come it's everybody else's fault that you're so miserable?

"Shut up," I said, glaring. "Just shut up."

She glared back.

"Okay, so maybe it is my fault. Maybe I am a big fat ugly pig all by myself."

She rolled her eyes. You must be a pig, she said. 'Cause you sure know how to wallow in it.

"Shut up," I said again. I looked away. She kept staring; I could feel her beady eyes on the back of my head. Finally I couldn't stand it. "What?" I yelled at her. "What do you want me to do?"

She narrowed her eyes.

"What?"

You know what.

"All right!" I threw my pillow at her. It missed, but cleared my dresser with a crash. I cringed, waiting for Mom and Dad to ax down the door with the rescue squad in tow. Nothing. I was saved.

From everyone but myself.

I sighed. It was a long, painful sigh. Then I got up and rummaged around in my backpack. "Where's that stupid food diary? Guess it's now or never."

There it was, in the bottom, under a half-empty box of Milk Duds. "So long, old pals. Parting is such sweet sorrow." Who said that? Shakespeare? What a turd. I tossed the Milk Duds in the trash.

I retrieved the diary and carried it to my bed. The

notebook seemed heavier than I remembered, especially since there was next to nothing written in it. Wait. Something was stuck to the back.

My eyes widened when I unstuck it.

Uh-oh. It was Lydia's science notebook. Melded to my food diary with sticky puffy paint.

Great, I thought. Tomorrow was going to be a double funeral. Harley's and mine. Because Lydia would kill me when she found out it was my fault she'd had to redo the science notebook. And everyone else would assist in the assassination since I'd spoiled our science project. So long, Harley. Good riddance, Jenny.

Chapter 21

"This is where I found him." Max stood beside the carcass of an old motorcycle and pointed to the ground. "This is where we'll bury him."

She handed Harley's shoe box coffin to Lydia while I handed Max the shovel. As Max dug, Prairie pulled out a miniature tape recorder from her book bag and said, "I brought some of my S-Sunday school music to play." She slid in a tape and hit the button. A rock version of "Jesus Loves Me" jolted us from our reverie.

The music was nice, even though it made my tears well up again. Church music always does that to me. Max stopped shoveling. She straightened her spine and stared down into the hole. For a few minutes, we all just stood and stared down into the hole. Then, over the background singers doo-wopping the finale, Max yelled, "It's time!"

Lydia started to hand the coffin to Max, then stopped. She said, "You were a great rat, Harley. An exceptional rat. Maybe the smartest rat in the world. Even though we didn't win the science prize, we'll never forget you."

"Amen," Prairie whispered.

Lydia turned and handed the box to Prairie. Prairie set the tape recorder down on a stack of car batteries and took the coffin. Closing her eyes, she moved her lips in a silent prayer to Harley. Then she handed the box to me.

I inhaled a long, shaky breath. No way could I say anything, silent or otherwise. A lump as huge as a hearse parked in my throat. Sniffling, I stared at the coffin. I had to say something. Everyone was waiting. At last I cleared my throat and croaked, "I have two confessions to make."

They all waited.

I swallowed hard, then said, "First, I'm the one who took your notebook, Lydia."

Her jaw dropped.

"I didn't mean to. It was an accident." I explained how it turned up last night attached to my food diary.

How I must've picked them both up that day in science when Mr. Krupps was there.

Lydia took the pink notebook from me and said, "I was so sure Ashley stole it."

"I know," I said. "I feel kinda bad about accusing her." Who would've guessed she'd actually been telling the truth when she'd played dumb? I mean, it'd be a first.

Lydia stared at the notebook, shaking her head. "But how did Ashley know about our project? About Harley and the Rat-o-rama?"

Prairie piped up, "How d-did she know so much about Hugh?"

Lydia and I both looked at Prairie. Then we eyeballed each other. "The survey!" we cried. Lydia riffled through her notebook. "It's gone. Ashley swiped it, right after she peeked at my science notes. I'd bet my life on it."

I wouldn't go that far. A super-size Snickers, maybe.

"Can we get on with this?" Max grumbled. She reached for the shoe box coffin.

"Wait." I held it back. "You haven't heard my second confession."

The air grew still. Stale. A fly buzzed around my ear, and I whapped it away.

"Well?" Max said. "Spit it out."

"I, uh . . ." I gulped. My throat was dry as desert dust. Squeezing my eyes closed, I whispered hoarsely, "I killed Harley."

This time three jaws unhinged.

"H-how?" Prairie asked.

"If I hadn't given him junk food for positive reinforcement, he might still be alive."

In unison they all went, "Huh?"

"Don't you know he died of obesity? Probably had a heart attack from all the cholesterol."

"Crapola," Max said.

I glanced over at her.

Prairie wrinkled her nose. "I d-doubt it, Jenny. It was just his time. It c-comes for all of us, you know."

I looked at Lydia. She didn't say anything.

My eyes welled with tears. In a moment I was going to start blubbering. "Maybe you should elect another leader," I said. "Somebody more . . . responsible."

"You're responsible."

Through tears I blinked up to see who'd spoken. Shock. It was Lydia. "Yeah," I muttered. "For Harley's death. For ruining our project."

"Crapola," Max said again.

"What I meant was you're responsible for all the

good stuff that happened," Lydia continued. "For getting our science project done on time. For assigning us duties and organizing us. You're responsible for all of us getting A's in science." She shoved her glasses up her nose. "My first A ever in science. My mother's going to cheer for a year. Maybe she'll even let me watch TV." Lydia grinned.

Prairie put in, "It's m-my first A in science, too."

Max mumbled, "My first A in anything. Ever."

Mine, too. A slow smile spread across my face. Thanks, guys, I thought. You're the best. I still felt a little responsible for Harley's death, though. Exhaling a long breath, I raised my eyes to the sky. "Harley," I said, "if you can hear me, say hi to Petey." I hoped that rats and hamsters shared rodent heaven.

I passed the coffin to Max. She stared at it for the longest time. I was sure she was going to start bawling. Instead, she set the shoe box on a stack of tires and said, "I wrote a poem."

She dug into her camouflage jacket pocket, pulled out a notebook, and flipped it open. In a husky voice, she read, " 'To Harley, The Wonder Rat.' " She cleared her throat.

" 'To others you were just a rat;
To us you were a wonder.

Better than a cat or bat,
A muskrat or a condor.
You were a friend,
The best I had;
I wish you lots of luck.
Compared to other friends I've had,
You're the best—
They suck.'

"No offense," Max said to us. "It's the only rhyme I could think of."

"None t-taken." Prairie sniffled.

Max lowered Harley into the grave. We each tossed a handful of dirt over the coffin. Lydia said in a wavery voice, "I m-made a marker." From her book bag, she pulled two silver chopsticks glued together in a cross. With purple puffy paint she'd spelled *Harley* on a hunk of cardboard hot-glued to the cross. Lydia stuck the cross in the ground at the head of the grave. Prairie had picked a handful of dandelions to sprinkle on top of the box. We all bowed our heads for a moment of silence. Then Prairie cranked up "Jesus Loves Me," and, tears streaming down our cheeks, we covered our little lost friend with dirt.

Chapter 22

When I dragged myself through the front door at home, my whole family was sitting in the living room. It was strange. The TV wasn't on or anything. Mom rose to her feet. "Jenny, I'm . . . we're"— she looked around —"so sorry about Harley."

"Harley's a rat," I said. "A dead rat."

Mom nodded. "We know."

I lost it. Mom rushed up and hugged me. Then Dad hugged me. Behind them came Vanessa.

Wow, a group hug. I couldn't believe it. Wiping tears from my eyes, I said, "How did you know?"

"A boy in your class called," Mom said.

My puffy eyes swelled. "Who? When?"

"Last night. Remember you got a call? He didn't

say who he was," Mom went on. "Just that he wanted to know how you were doing. He told us what happened at the science fair. How upset you were."

Hugh. Great.

"Why didn't you tell us about Harley, Jenny?" Dad asked.

I sagged and shrugged. "I didn't think you'd understand." Then the truth. "I didn't think you'd care."

"Of course we care," Mom said. "We're your family."

"Could've fooled me."

Everyone dropped their arms. The hair on my neck tingled, like the air was about to burst into flames. Vanessa met my eyes. She clucked her tongue. I clucked back. She clucked twice. I clucked three times. We both cracked up. Then we all dissolved into hysterics.

When I regained composure, I whispered to Van, "We still on for tonight?"

She whispered back, "If you feel like it."

A slow smile spread across my face. "Mom, Dad"—I turned to them—"would you guys mind leaving for about an hour?"

They shared a shocked look.

"Take a ride," I said. "Go up to Inspiration Point."

"Jenny!" Mom dropped her jaw.

Dad smiled at Mom. "We haven't been up there in ages."

"Robert!" Mom slapped his arm. "It's still light out."

Dad chuckled. "The better to see you with, my dear." He wiggled his eyebrows.

Beside me, Vanessa muttered, "I think I'm going to be sick."

I pushed our parents out the door to the garage. "One hour," I reminded them.

After making sure they were safely out of sight, I caught up with Vanessa in the kitchen. "Did you get everything?" I asked her.

She nodded. "You go find the good dishes and silver. I'll cook."

This should be good, I thought. I hoped Mom and Dad wouldn't come back hungry. Vanessa added, "And don't forget the candles."

An hour later, Mom and Dad walked in on a romantic candlelight dinner. They both just stood in the doorway and stared.

"Sit here, *Madame*," I said, ushering Mom to her chair. "*Monsieur*." I escorted Dad.

While Vanessa dished up this stroganoff stuff she'd learned to make in home economics, I poured the champagne. Okay, it wasn't real champagne, just diet Sprite, but it was bubbly and I threw in a maraschino cherry to make it fancy.

We lit the candles and dimmed the lights. Then Vanessa and I bowed out to the basement. "Call us when you're ready for dessert," I said, easing the door closed behind me.

We played darts for about an hour. "It's awful quiet," I finally said. "What do you think they're doing up there?"

Vanessa hit a bull's-eye. "What do you think?"

My eyes bulged. "In the kitchen?"

She aimed a dart at me. Suddenly we heard music seeping through the floorboards. It wasn't music, exactly. It was the twang of a banjo, the yowl of a yodel.

"Oh, no," I said. "You know how Dad hates to dance."

Vanessa eyed the ceiling, looking worried. "We better break it up before they get in a big argument."

We charged up the stairs. On the landing, Vanessa stopped me with a stiff arm. With her other hand, she held a finger to her lips. She opened the door slowly, and we both peered in.

It was dark. The only light came from the flickering candles on the kitchen table. The table where no one was sitting.

"Where'd they go?" I whispered. Then we heard the music drift in from the living room. This time it wasn't country, or if it was, it sounded like a simple, soft ballad. Over the lilting melody, we heard Mom giggle.

Vanessa looked at me. We both must've inherited the same curiosity gene, because we couldn't tiptoe to the living room fast enough.

There they were, dancing together to a love song on the stereo. Mom's head rested on Dad's shoulder. And they both had the same expression on their faces, probably the one I get whenever I dream about me and Kevin Rooney together. Except their expressions were sweeter because this wasn't a dream.

Chapter 23

Monday before school, the four of us, the Snob Squad, squatted on the baseball bleachers, sharing a breakfast bar. I pulled out my food diary to record the moment. For Minnette. For me. Yeah, I decided to go back to her. Even though I realized my eating problem was mine to solve, I really felt I needed her help and support. Everyone needs help and support sometimes. Problems can get too big for one person to handle.

Or even two people. Mom and Dad had told us over breakfast that they were going to keep seeing Dr. Sid for counseling. They were determined to work through their problems. And ours. Then they'd told us they loved and appreciated us — all that mushy stuff. Stuff we hated to hear. Stuff we needed to hear. Vanessa had rolled her eyes, but I'd noticed she'd snarfed down two whole muffins while we'd been talking, while I barely took a bite of mine.

"Lydia"—I turned to her suddenly—"do me a favor. Every time I eat something, remind me to write it in my food diary."

"Sure, okay," she said, sounding surprised.

I knew Lydia wouldn't forget. "And the rest of you guys, too. You've got to help me with this diet. One for all . . . ?"

"And all for one," they finished. We slapped palms.

Sometimes leadership means knowing when to lead, and sometimes it means knowing when to ask your team for help.

Prairie slumped and sighed. It was a different sigh, a long, drawn-out one. A sigh pocked with pain.

"What is it, Prairie?" I said. "Does something hurt?"

"M-my foot," she replied. "It's killing me."

"Can't you oil it or something?" Lydia asked.

We all looked at Lydia.

"What?" she said.

Prairie answered, "I'm g-getting a new prosthesis.

This one's too small. But my n-new one w-won't be in for a couple more weeks." She punched at her ankle. "I can't stand it. Do you guys mind? I have to t-take it off for a while."

"Go ahead," we all said.

"I can't look." Lydia turned her head.

"Wuss," Max muttered.

Max and I watched while Prairie slid the plastic leg down out of her jeans. Not out completely, just enough so that her feet weren't even when she stretched out her legs. "Ah, b-better." Her head lolled back.

At that moment two people emerged from behind the baseball dugout. "Jenny!" one of them called.

I steeled for an attack. Habit, I guess.

It was Kevin and Hugh. As they approached, my muscles relaxed, except for my heart. It skipped a beat. Then my eyes met Hugh's, and my stomach lurched. Oh, God. Did he really like me? Was he actually going to ask me to the dance?

Kevin spoke first. "We're really sorry about what happened Saturday," he said.

"Yeah," Hugh added. "That was one amazing rat."

We all bowed our heads. Lydia said, "We had a funeral yesterday. You should've come."

"Yeah?" Kevin said. "We would've. You should've told us."

The conversation stalled. From my bent head, I stole a glance at Kevin. He kicked a rock. Hugh scratched his armpit. He said, "Say, is that your prosthesis, Prairie?" He pointed to her foot.

We all cringed. Beside me Max stood. Her fists clenched.

Prairie said, "Y-yes. I t-took it off because it p-pinches."

"Could I see?" Hugh hunkered down.

Max growled.

"S-sure," Prairie said. She started to pull up the leg of her jeans.

Lydia grasped my shoulder. "I think I'm going to be sick."

Saved by the bell. Literally. I jumped up, hauling Lydia to her feet.

Max threatened Hugh with a snarl on her way past, and he looked at her with an expression like "What? What'd I do?"

We turned to head for class. Lydia pulled up beside me. Prairie said, "I'll be along." She handed the leg to Hugh.

Hugh, cradling the plastic prosthesis like a newborn

baby, said, "It's heavier than I thought. It must be hard to walk."

"You get u-used to it," Prairie said. "Except this one's too small. I'm g-getting a new one."

"Yeah?" Hugh's eyebrows arched. "Could I have your old one?"

"Oh, gag." Lydia stuck out her tongue.

While the three of us sauntered slowly toward the temp building, I peered over my shoulder. Hugh examined every inch of Prairie's leg. "Wow," I heard him say. "Can you dance?"

Lydia gripped my arm. "I heard," I said.

Prairie said, "Yes. Why?"

Max yanked me toward the building, which pulled Lydia along since she was permanently attached to my arm. Luckily our ears were tuned in because we heard Hugh say, "I wanted to ask you a question, Prairie."

Lydia squealed in my ear, which prevented any further attempt at eavesdropping since I was now deaf. "See, I told you he wouldn't go with Ashley," she said. "Didn't I tell you?"

"Yeah, you told me." Guess that meant he wasn't going with me, either. Which was a relief. And a disappointment, surprisingly. "Would you please let go of my arm?" I said.

Lydia frowned. "I'm not holding your arm anymore." She stepped back.

My head twisted, and as it did, my eyes zoomed right into Kevin Rooney's. "Could I talk to you a second, Jenny?" he said. "Alone?" He looked at Lydia, who was hyperventilating in my face.

I said to Max, "I'll catch up." It was a miracle how I could utter three coherent words at a moment like this.

Max glanced at Kevin, then me. "Yell if you need me," she said. She veered toward the temp building, Lydia in tow.

When they were gone, Kevin said, "I called you yesterday."

I almost didn't hear him through the rushing of blood to my ears. "You did? How did you get my num—" Hugh. That's why Hugh asked Prairie for my number? To give to Kevin? Okay, Jenny. Be cool, I ordered myself. My blood pressure soared. Any minute I was going to start hemorrhaging.

"Listen, I was wondering," he said. "Well, I mean I was wondering how you were. After Harley . . . you know. After he . . . you seemed pretty upset."

He'd noticed. How could he not notice a total emotional meltdown in public? "Yeah, well, you would be, too, if your prize rat just keeled over and died." And you figured it was your fault, I didn't add.

"I guess *so*," he said.

"Max took it hardest, though. Harley was her rat."

Kevin nodded. "I wanted to talk to you after the science fair, but with the crowd and all the commotion . . ." He scraped a circle in the gravel with the toe guard of his Reebok. "It isn't fair that they disqualified you for using a live animal in your project."

"No kidding. Especially since he was dead."

"I didn't mean—" When he saw me smiling, Kevin chuckled.

The second bell rang, and we hustled toward the temp. On the way he told me what a cool project ours was and how stupid his was. "Barbie and Ken. Brother." He rolled his eyes.

"So, that barfing we heard coming from Ken. Was that your contribution?" I asked.

Kevin smirked.

If barf can be adorable, his was.

"We never should've let Ashley and Melanie take over the project." Kevin shifted his backpack to his outside shoulder. "We spent more time figuring out what the computers were going to wear than we did getting them to work."

"I especially liked the mustache on Ken. Nice touch."

Kevin elbowed me.

God, he touched me. I'd never wash my arm again.

At the steps to the temp building, Kevin stopped. He removed something from his pack and said, "Here, this is yours." He handed it to me.

I looked at it and freaked. My glamour photo. The worst one, too. The one where I was trying to act all sexy and everything. Groaning, I clutched the picture to my chest. My heaving chest. How long had he had this? A week? Why was it all bent? And why was there a little hole in the top?

"It doesn't really look like you," he said.

"Who does it look like?" I frowned. "Don't answer that."

He smiled. "No, I mean you look better in person." He blushed. Or else he had a sudden bout of indigestion. I know I did.

Kevin started up the steps. Turning back, he said, "You going to the dance on Friday?"

"I dunno," I said through shock. "Why?"

He stared off over my head. "Just wondered."

"You going?"

He raked his hand through his gorgeous hair. "I might go. I mean, even Hugh's going." He sort of rolled his eyes.

"Where Hugh goes, you goes?"

He laughed. And looked at me.

"Sorry." My eyes dropped.

"Well." His hand poised on the doorknob. "If I do go, will you go? With me, I mean?"

"Sure." I gulped an ocean. "Since Prairie's going."

He exhaled a long breath. "Great. That wasn't so hard. At least she said yes."

He wasn't talking to me. He was talking to air. Not air, exactly. Kevin Rooney was talking to himself. How adorable. It made me laugh.

"What?" he said.

"Nothing." I shook my head.

Then we both cracked up.

Friday, I thought, as I squeezed past Kevin through the door that he held open for me. I'd have to lose twenty pounds by Friday. "Right," I muttered. Maybe two pounds would be a good start. The way Kevin was smiling at me, I already felt as light as angel food cake.